BOMBER

WAR BROTHERS MC

BIANCA LEE WARD

This book contains adult themes and is not suitable for persons under the age of 18.

For information regarding possible triggers, please see www.biancaleeward.com or contact info@biancaleeward.com.

First published in 2023 by Bianca Lee

Bomber

<u>Copyright</u> © Bianca Lee Ward 2023

The moral rights of the author have been asserted.

All rights reserved.

Copyright Notice: No part of this book may be reproduced or transmitted in any form or by any means, electronic or mechanical, including photocopying and recording, or by any information storage and retrieval system, without permission in writing from the publisher.

This is a work of fiction. Names, places, characters, and incidents are the product of the author's imagination or are used fictitiously, and any resemblance to any actual persons, living or dead, organizations, events, or locales is entirely coincidental.

Warning: The unauthorized reproduction or distribution of this copyrighted work is illegal.

Cover Photo: Shutterstock

Cover Designer: Emily at www.quirkycirce.com.au

ALSO BY BIANCA LEE WARD

REAPER

War Brothers MC

I let her go once because she wasn't mine.

This time, I'll die before I give her up . . .

I want her.

That smile . . . those curves.

But Ava doesn't belong to me.

Then she arrives in my clubhouse, seeking refuge. My gut churns at the sight of the bruises on her face, the fear in her eyes.

Before I was the president of the War Brothers Motorcycle Club, I was a sniper in the military who hunted down evil men like her husband. Now I avoid relationships because the wounds I have are more than skin deep.

But Ava's different, and when I find her in the wrong bedroom—my bedroom—one night, what happens next changes everything.

I let her go once because she was married, but I won't make the same mistake twice.

I'll die before I let her dangerous husband, the jealous women in our club, or the enemy our club didn't see coming lay a finger on her.

Because this time around, Ava is mine.

Grab your copy of Reaper now.

VIPER

War Brothers MC

I've got one month to convince her to be my wife . . .

Until I laid eyes on Sophie, I never planned on marriage. All that changed after our hot night together in Vegas.

Now she regrets our impulsive Vegas wedding and is demanding a divorce. But I'm not signing the papers. Hell no! I'll give up every single one of my womanizing ways for a woman like her.

Sophie thinks I'm only infatuated by her looks, except I see how everyone underestimates her. I'm not intimidated by her wealth, her modeling career, and the trail of broken hearts she has left behind. What we have is different.

I've lived my whole life unable to feel anything thanks to my rough childhood, but for Sophie I'll risk everything. Her rich father and the jealous women in my club aren't going to stand in my way.

If she wants a divorce, she'll have to spend one month with me at the War Brothers clubhouse. Sleeping in my bed.

Then we'll see if she still refuses to say I do . . .

Grab your copy of Viper now.

PLAYLIST

Glass House – Machine Gun Kelly feat. Naomi Wild
Bleed For You – Our Last Night
Broken – Seether feat. Amy Lee
Last Resort (Reimagined) – Falling in Reverse
Never Know – Bad Omens
Searchlights – The Brave
Without You – The Kid Laroi
Alone – I Prevail
My Blood – Ellie Goulding, Iykyk, Ida More & Ky Karter
Ghost – Pink is Punk & Benny Benassi
Memories – Maroon 5
Wake Me Up – Avicii
Runaway – Linkin Park
By Myself – Linkin Park
Sunrise – Our Last Night
Nothing Inside – Machine Gun Kelly feat. Iann Dior
Just Pretend – Bad Omens
Heavy – Linkin Park feat. Kiiara
Figure.09 – Linkin Park
Battle Scars – Guy Sebastian
It's Not Over – Daughtry
Drag Me Down – One Direction
The Death of Peace of Mind – Bad Omens
After All – Culture Code, ARAYA & RUNN
One More Light – Linkin Park
Coming Home – Diddy feat. Skylar Grey
I'll Be Missing You – Puff Daddy & Faith Evans
Gasoline – I Prevail
Breakaway – Kelly Clarkson

Sometimes love needs to struggle in the darkness to
transform into something beautiful.

BEST
FRIENDS

ONE
EIGHTEENTH BIRTHDAY PARTY

Zara
   Age: Eighteen

"Happy birthdayyyyy to you."

I peer over my bowl of cornflakes to see Misty with a wide grin and a gleam in her eyes.

"Happy birthday to you," she sings as she walks closer to me, her hands behind her back. "Happy birthday to my best friend and sister, Zara"—she takes a deep breath—"happy birthday to youuuu." As she's opera singing the last few notes, Misty passes me a pink envelope.

I smile at her. "You didn't have to get me anything."

She hisses. "Yes, I did!"

I jump off my chair and wrap my arms around her, squeezing her tightly. "Thank you."

She pulls back and stares at the envelope. "Come on, open it."

"Okay, okay." I slide my fingers underneath the flap of the envelope to rip it open, then glide the card out.

The front has a love heart, and inside it says "You will always be the sister of my soul and the friend of my heart."

"Aww." I grin, feeling touched. I open the card and two small rectangular pieces of paper land on the table. I put down the card and pick them up to see Sun Dance festival tickets.

I lift my eyes to hers. "How did you get these? I thought they were sold out?"

"I have my sources," she replies.

Which basically means Knox and Kane's mom, Audrey Crown, pulled strings to get them for us. Her family founded Crown Village—where we live—and owns every successful business in it. Her reach has no bounds.

Crown Village is a coastal town packed with amenities: beaches, a lake, restaurants, a resort, a casino, and a park. It has a small population and a tight-knit community for the people who reside here, but it's also a holiday attraction for the rich and famous.

"The guys are taking us in the limo, and since the festival is at the amusement park, I thought we could go on a couple of rides before DJ Mesah comes on."

I clap my hands in excitement—Mesah is our favorite DJ.

"Mesah's playing at noon, so we'll at least get to see her set and some of the DJs after her. We'll be home in time for your party . . . where we can have some drinks."

My eyes dart to the entryway of the kitchen, checking no one had heard. "I wouldn't be saying that out loud if I were you."

We're lucky if Mom allows us to have a glass of champagne *in her presence*, let alone whatever strong alcohol Misty has conned Kane into getting.

"But aren't you still sick?" I heard her retching this morning. She hasn't been able to get rid of whatever illness she has.

"I told you something I've been eating hasn't been sitting

well with me." She shrugs. "I don't know. My body hates me. Anyway . . . enough about that. I think you may have forgotten something." Her eyes latch back onto the envelope.

Lifting the envelope, I feel there's still something inside. I tip it upside down to see a silver necklace drop into my hand. It has a charm on it, half a heart that says *Friends*. Misty's hand goes to her neck, and she pulls a similar chain from outside of her top to show me that her part says *Best*.

"I know it's lame, but I saw it and I had to have it."

I roll my eyes as I pass the necklace to her and lift my long hair. "Can you put it on?"

She drapes the necklace around my neck, and I feel the cold metal against my skin.

"There," she says.

I let my hair fall down my back and gently tug on the necklace, feeling it's secure.

Iris walks in. "Happy eighteenth," she says in a sing-song voice.

"Thank you!" I reply.

Iris, who's in her fifties and from the Philippines, has been working for us since Misty and I were little. She helps around the house three days a week with cleaning, laundry, cooking, and looking after us. She's petite, with an exotic appearance—black hair, olive skin, and dark-brown oval eyes.

"What cake would you like for tonight?" Iris asks.

I salivate as I think about it.

Misty snorts. "I thought you would have made the cake by now."

Iris narrows her eyes, but her lip twitches like she's smothering a smile. "I can't, and it's because of you, that's why!"

Misty's mouth falls open. Her hand goes to her chest. "Who! Me?"

"Yes, you! You little pig!"

Misty's cackle is loud. She turns to me, then makes a point of snorting even louder.

Iris laughs. "You can't help yourself. I wasn't baking two cakes because you couldn't keep your hands off of it."

"It's not my fault!" she complains.

Iris's brows lift high on her forehead. "Then whose fault is it?"

"Yours!"

Mom walks through the kitchen as I'm giggling, listening to them bicker.

"Happy birthday, sweetheart," Mom says before walking to me and placing a tender kiss on my forehead.

I smile at her.

"Your father said to say happy birthday. Something came up at work this morning, but he said he'll come home when he can."

I bob my head in acknowledgment. Then my attention drifts back to Misty and Iris.

"How is it my fault?" Iris asks.

"You're a damn good cook. I've had really bad cravings lately. I just can't resist your food."

Iris laughs and places her hand on Misty's head, then messes up her hair.

"Hey!" Misty whines as she attempts to flatten it.

"Can I have a chocolate cake, but with a layer of chocolate cream and fresh strawberries?" I ask Iris.

"That sounds yummy!" Misty chimes in.

"I'll go get the ingredients this morning," Iris replies. She turns to Mom. "Do you need anything else for tonight?"

"Audrey's organized catering for the party, so we should be fine. But thank you." Mom turns to me. "You'll have to wait to get your birthday present from us when your dad gets home."

Knox and Kane barge into the kitchen like it's their own

home. Our parents were really tight and our families were inseparable. But then, things changed when their parents split. However, it didn't mess up our bond with the boys—or the connection between Misty and Kane or me and Knox. We're all still as close as ever!

My eyes wander up and down Knox's body. He's wearing a fitted black shirt that shows off his chest and broad shoulders, ripped black jeans, and black boots. Knox is that total package of deliciousness. It's not just his face and build that draw me to him but also that bad-boy swagger he wears so well. That moody behavior he has toward everyone except me.

Knox's eyes lock onto mine. He strides over until he is flush against my back and folds his arms around me. He bows his head and nuzzles my neck, making goose bumps travel along my arms.

"Happy birthday," he says in my ear.

My chest warms. "Thank you."

"Happy birthday!" Kane yells, his larger-than-life personality on show.

The Hart brothers look similar with their signature whiskey-colored eyes, but their personalities differ. Kane is all smiles and mischief; Knox is broody and intense. While Kane is easygoing, Knox is distant and quiet.

Even their clothing sense is different. Knox is mostly in black and might wear something white for contrast, whereas Kane is usually dressed in bright fashionable T-shirts with matching-color, branded sneakers.

Knox's arms slip away from me. I turn to see him pull a small jewelry case from his back pocket. When he places it in my hand, I touch the soft velvet material of the lid before opening it to see a large blue emerald-cut crystal surrounded by tiny diamonds. I clutch my chest as I suck in a breath through my teeth.

I feel a hand on my shoulder. I glance to the side and see Misty. She whistles.

My hands tremble. I open my mouth to speak, but I can't. A deep chuckle comes from Kane. Knox gently takes the case from my hands, and I watch as he pulls the ring out and then slides it onto the fourth finger on my right hand.

I thought someone would purchase a ring for my birthday. Misty wasn't very subtle in going to the jewelry store, trying on different rings, and measuring my size while we were there.

"Mom told me the band is platinum and the big crystal is a sapphire. The crystals around it are diamonds . . ." He rubs the back of his neck, suddenly shy. "It's a family heirloom."

A range of emotions strike me at once—happiness, appreciation—but I also worry that I'll lose it. It looks expensive. I rise onto my toes and give him a chaste kiss on the lips.

"Where's my diamond-and-sapphire ring?" Misty taunts Kane before elbowing him in the ribs.

He coughs, then caresses his side where she elbowed him. "Maybe you can get a ring next year."

Mom and Iris hover around me, so I turn and hold my ring out to them, feeling giddy and spoiled.

"Oh my . . ." Mom says. She looks at Knox before looking back at the ring. "It's absolutely stunning."

Iris tugs on my hand, pulling it closer to her. "For heaven's sake, child, don't lose it."

I bring my hand back to my side and lean into Knox. "Thank you."

He kisses my temple. "You're welcome, precious."

"How about we go get changed?" Misty suggests.

On the way to our bedrooms, Misty halts and turns to me with a deep frown. "You don't have to wear the necklace I got you. It looks so lame compared to the ring Knox gave you."

My heart aches for her. I lift my hand and hold the necklace charm in my palm, as if I'm protecting it from Misty's cruel words.

"Please don't say that. I love it."

Misty is an extrovert, but there are moments like this when I can see her insecurities.

Although my family is well-off, our wealth pales in comparison to what Audrey Knox, and Kane's mother, inherited from her family. I gather Misty paid for the necklace herself.

My dad is an accountant at Crown-Hart Casino, which was owned by Knox and Kane's parents, but their dad, David, got it and the house in the divorce. Although Audrey kept all the assets she inherited from her family and their holiday houses, David got the casino on the condition that Knox and Kane would be a part of the business and inherit it once David passes, though I get the feeling Knox isn't interested in it.

Misty gives me a small smile before she enters her bedroom.

After I get changed into shorts and a shirt, the sound of someone clearing their throat makes me hastily turn. Mom is standing awkwardly by my bed.

"You scared me." After I get over my shock, I ask, "What's wrong?"

Mom looks at the floor before staring at me. "Do we have to have *the talk*?"

My eyebrows furrow. "What talk?"

"*The* talk. Now that you're eighteen."

My stomach drops. "Mom, no! The talk is not needed."

"Should I take you to the doctor to put you on the pill?"

"Mom!" I cringe and my cheeks burn from embarrassment.

"Well, I'm here if you ever want to talk about it or go to the doctor."

I attempt to smile at her in thanks and wait for her to leave the room. I wait ten more minutes to ensure that I'm not bright red before I walk downstairs.

An hour later, the limousine arrives. We travel through the suburban part of town, toward the amusement park on the main strip of road close to Crown Beach.

Excitement shoots through me—I love the amusement park. We're always guaranteed a good time, and Misty and I both see it as our happy place. It's where Knox and I and Misty and Kane had our first double date. The restaurant, with its ocean view, is where our families have celebrated special occasions over the years.

We walk to the available ticket booth. When the worker sees us, his eyes widen.

"I'm Zara. This is Misty," I glance between the guys. "This is Knox and Kane. Their mother is Audrey Crown. We're here to get the VIP passes."

The employee blinks a few times, then pushes his glasses up his nose. He looks at Knox and shuffles back in his seat like he's scared of him. His colleague, who has finished serving a family at the next window, looks over and says, "Billy, the Crowns own the amusement park. Just give them the VIP passes."

The guy turns away, picks up the passes, and places them on the counter. He clears his throat. "Have a good day."

As we walk through the clown-face entryway, I'm greeted by a variety of carnival music and laughter. In the distance is the top of the red-and-white Ferris wheel, and to my right is a large roller coaster.

As we walk toward the food shops, the scent of coffee wafts to me first, followed by the smell of something oily and deep fried. Then I smell popcorn and candy floss, which makes my stomach rumble.

"I want ice cream. You want some?" Misty asks, her eyes darting between the three of us.

"Yes, please," I answer.

"Kane, come help me carry them back." He moans under his breath but follows her to the ice cream stand.

Misty and Kane stroll back to us and hand us our ice cream.

"Can you hold mine for a second?" Misty asks me with a wicked glimmer in her eye.

She hands me her ice cream cone and glances at Kane. When he brings the ice cream up to lick it, her hand bolts out and she smashes it into his face.

Misty, Knox, and I burst out in laughter as Kane stands and blinks a few times with his mouth open wide. Chocolate ice cream is everywhere—all over his face, even in his eyes. It drips off his face onto his shirt.

The shock evaporates, and a slow, evil grin paints Kane's face. Within seconds, he hurls himself at Misty, who screams. He rubs his head on her neck, spreading the ice cream into her hair.

It isn't long before Misty's in the bathroom cleaning herself up while cursing Kane.

I put my hand under the tap and then run my fingers through her hair to try to get the stickiness out. "You're not going to get all of this out now."

She whines loudly, still trying to rub her shirt with water. "I give up. I want to go on the rides before DJ Mesah starts."

When we return to the guys, Misty checks her watch. "Okay, we have time to go on two rides. What to choose, what to choose?"

She wiggles her eyebrows at us, exaggerating the hard choice, but we know what she'll choose. "Bumper cars to make the guys happy." She gives me a pointed look. "And our favorite, the carousel?"

Kane groans. "What is with you two and the carousel? It's a kids' ride."

Misty has been dragging me on the carousel since we were young kids. It's our thing.

Misty snorts at Kane. "Funny, because you're the biggest kid here."

He rolls his eyes. "What about the sledgehammer or big dipper roller coaster?"

Both being thrill rides, I'm not surprised he chose them.

"No. Fair is fair. Bumper cars for all of us and then the carousel because it's Zara's birthday. Better watch yourself on the bumper cars, Kane," she taunts.

Kane flashes her a roguish smile. "Bring it on."

We climb into our bumper cars. My gaze cuts to the others and I grin at them in excitement. I grip the steering wheel as I focus in front of me. When the green light flashes, Misty and Kane ram each other. Misty cackles.

As I'm watching them, I see Knox aiming for me. I turn and go as fast as I can to get away from him while a woman and child in one car bump into him, which turns him away from me. I smile back at him in victory.

After our time finishes, we get out of the bumper cars. Knox takes my hand, and we take the steps down to the ground, where we make our way past the small kids' roller coaster and the spinning teacups.

The next is the carousel, with its gold crest and range of horses and carts. Kane and Knox wait outside as Misty and I show our VIP pass to the man operating the ride. We step up to the platform and weave between the seats until she finds a horse rearing up on its back legs. I get onto one that looks as though it's galloping. Misty swings her leg over and hops on. She holds on with one hand, peers over her shoulder, and smiles at me.

Soon after we finish the ride, we walk to the large event.

We show our tickets to the ticket collector. Once inside, the noise is earsplitting.

"I want to get up to the front," Misty calls out. Kane nods, grabs her hand, and pushes through the crowd. Misty clutches my wrist and pulls me along, while Knox steps to my side and helps me get through the bustle.

As we get closer, my heartbeat speeds up.

"Hello, everyone," DJ Mesah says into the microphone.

People cheer, and we keep shuffling. We cannot stop bumping into the mountains of people crammed inside, though there's a genuinely happy vibe in the crowd.

"I'd like to thank all of you for coming, and I hope you enjoy the set."

Misty and I cheer. We end up in the center about five people back from the barricade near the stage.

The music starts, and people lift their phones, videoing. The intro of the song starts slowly as the lights around the stage flash. When the beat kicks in, green lasers flicker through the crowd. The atmosphere of joy and excitement sends a chill down my spine.

The tempo increases, and then the beat drops. The chorus makes the crowd erupt in yells and cheers. Misty and I jump to the beat, our arms up. The guys are flush against us, protecting us from the rowdy people.

Half an hour in, Misty freezes. When I look at her, her hands are covering her mouth and she has paled significantly.

"Do you want to go?" I yell over the music.

Her eyes stretch wide and she frantically nods.

I turn to the guys and tap them on the arms. "We need to go now. Misty looks sick," I say loudly over the music.

Knox's and Kane's eyes flash with understanding. Knox walks ahead, creating room for us to move through the crowd. Once we make it through, Misty runs to the bathroom stalls.

My eyes flicker between Knox and Kane. "Can one of you call the limousine to pick us up? We'd better go home so Misty can get some rest before tonight."

MY HEART RACES AS I LOOK IN THE MIRROR. I HATE BEING THE center of attention. I wipe my sweaty hands on my dress.

"Zara. Marie. Pratt," Mom says. "For the love of all that is holy, do not wipe anything on that dress."

I flinch, then straighten my back. "Sorry, Mom."

When I saw this dress, I wanted it, but now I feel a sliver of guilt that it might have cost too much. I was so giddy when I saw it that I didn't even look at the price tag. It's a gold floor-length gown with a sweetheart neckline and sequins around the top half. I went with natural makeup and kept my hair simple by straightening it.

Misty steps into my bedroom and wolf whistles.

I stifle a laugh and swat at her. "You look pretty too."

Rarely does Misty grace us in a dress. She's wearing a floor-length green mermaid dress with a V neckline that makes her blue eyes pop. Her long blond hair is half up in waves.

"How are you feeling? You don't have to celebrate tonight. I understand if you want to go back to bed and rest."

"Actually, I'm feeling a little better," she replies.

"My girls are beautiful tonight," Mom says, her voice cracking at the end.

Misty and I may not share the same blood, but she is my sister. Our parents adopted Misty because they didn't think they could conceive, but Mom fell pregnant soon after adopting Misty as a newborn, which is why we are so close in age.

"Don't get too excited. Look at these bad boys," Misty says as she lifts her dress, revealing socks and black-and-white Vans.

Giggling at her, I shake my head and sneak a peek at Mom. She's glaring at Misty, but then her shoulders drop an inch, as if she's defeated. She knows as well as anyone that when Misty has made her mind up, nothing can change it.

Mom sighs. "Can you at least keep the dress down so no one can see your shoes?"

Misty looks up as if considering her response. "I can do that," she says with a smirk.

"The guests are arriving."

I turn to see Iris by the bedroom door. She rarely works this late but offered to stay back and help. My birthday wouldn't be the same without her here. She's like family.

Iris's eyes dart between me and Misty, and she fans her face like she's trying not to cry.

"Not you too?" I say. My family's overly emotional today.

She holds up her palm to me. "I need a minute."

Knox and Kane's mom, Audrey, walks in past Iris. She claps. "Family photos. I have the photographer ready downstairs."

Audrey's wearing a long, elegant dark-blue dress and a necklace with large round diamonds, which glisten in the light.

The uninterested look on Misty's face makes me laugh.

"Do we have to do photos too?" she whines.

"Misty . . ." Mom warns. "Before I know it, you two will be out of the house, living your own lives. It won't kill you to smile for a couple of photos."

Audrey steps closer to me. "Stunning." She peers down at the ring on my finger, and her lips curve higher.

I smile back in appreciation.

Audrey glances at Misty, who pulls up her dress to show

off her shoes to try get a rise out of Audrey. It works—Audrey's face twists in disgust.

Audrey and I have always had a strong bond, but there's been some tension between Audrey and Misty. They're polite, but they're not exactly best friends. Audrey doesn't approve of Misty's behavior and rebellious attitude. And because of that, she's not thrilled about her son Kane dating Misty.

"Thank you. Are Knox and Kane here yet?" Anticipation at seeing Knox dressed up thrums through my veins.

"Yes, they are. Photos first!" Audrey warns. She knows me and Misty well.

Mom steps over to Audrey. "I can't thank you enough for helping to make this a special day for Zara."

"Helen, stop! I am your daughter's godmother. Organizing this was easy." Audrey shoos Mom away and swings her head toward us. "Girls, downstairs."

We walk out of my bedroom and down the stairs to see Dad waiting for us at the bottom. When he sees us, a smile envelops his face. He spreads his arms wide, and when I reach the bottom stair, I step into them.

"Happy birthday," he says when he pulls back out of the hug. "The both of you look beautiful."

"Thanks, Dad," Misty replies.

I peer around at the subtle mix of gold, black, and white decorations. The photo booth is adorned with *18* in gold balloons.

Iris walks past before Mom and Audrey arrive. Audrey steps in front of us and points to the man holding a camera. "The photographer will be taking photos all night, but we should do a formal family one before Helen gets into the wine."

Dad laughs.

Mom scoffs. "That's pretty rich coming from you."

Audrey's head falls back as she laughs. "I've got us some lovely bottles of champagne."

"Can we get this over and done with? You alcoholics can get back to chatting about your wine afterward."

I nod with Misty.

Audrey walks further into the center of the house. She points to a backdrop under the chandelier, where all the photography lights are set up. We follow her lead.

"Zara first, by herself, then Misty, Zara, and the family."

I step into the middle of the equipment and follow the instructions, smiling and trying my best not to blink every time the bright light flashes.

After the family photos are finished, I pose for one photo with Audrey.

"Iris," I call out. She's talking to a server and looks up when she hears me call. "Please come and take a photo with me."

Iris's eyes widen. She says something to the server and makes her way to me. "I'd love to have my photo taken with you." She's beaming.

I wrap my arm around her and smile into the camera.

When we finish, I see Misty standing with Kane and Knox. I start walking toward them, but I hear Mom calling my name.

"Come and see your birthday present." She tilts her head toward the front of the house.

My stomach flutters. "Where is it?"

"Your present is outside."

My heart thumps in my chest, and all I can think is, *Please be a car, please be a car . . .*

Dashing toward the front door, I pass Audrey's security guard, and Mom giggles behind me. I pull the door open wide, my eyes scanning the driveway. Dad is next to a small white Mercedes Benz. I squeal and rush to it. It beeps and flashes when I reach it, and I turn to Dad, who is holding out the key.

I jump into his arms. "Thank you." I step to Mom and hug her.

"I hope you like it." Mom beams.

It's a hatchback, and it has a big Mercedes Benz logo in chrome on the grill.

"I love it!"

They smile at my eagerness, though Mom takes the car key from Dad. "You can have the key tomorrow. Now it's time to celebrate."

TWO
SHE'S MY WORLD

Knox

Age: Eighteen

"Oh, baby, I can't wait to rip this dress off of you."

I groan. I don't want to hear that. I look at Kane and Misty. "Get a room, would you?"

They smile at me. "You don't have to tell me twice," Kane says, grabbing Misty's hand and striding away.

I shake my head. My sarcasm was lost on them. I search the room, checking that Zara hasn't walked in and seen them bolt upstairs. I hate knowing something she doesn't. Kane told me they're sleeping together, but Misty is yet to tell Zara. I don't understand what the delay is.

Scanning the room again, I see Dad, who has stepped through the front door. My mom is off to the side, talking to her bodyguard. When she sees Dad, her lips tighten and she shifts, turning her back to him.

At least Dad has tried to be friendly in their divorce. Mom's been a bitch toward him, and it annoys me because

Dad let it slip that Mom was the one having the affair. It should be Dad who's angry with her, not the other way round. If I were to guess . . . it's the guard who's by her side all the time.

Zara became my air through my parents' divorce. As my mom's son, I enjoy advantages like chauffeured limousines, unrestricted access to money, luxurious mansions, and lavish holidays. But I would gladly trade it all for a genuinely happy family life. Kane and I have always felt like members of the Pratt family, thanks to Zara's parents, Helen and John, who treat us as if we were their own kin.

Dad sees John and walks toward him. When they meet, they shake hands. I go to them.

"Hey, Dad, did you see Zara?"

He smiles. "Hey, yes. I met her outside."

"Everyone's arriving, so Zara's outside with her mom, greeting everyone. That was my opportunity to let them do their thing and get myself a whiskey," John says. He holds up a glass of honey-colored liquid.

"All I can say is good luck, son," Dad says to me.

I cock my head. "Good luck with what?"

His eyes mock me. "Zara's getting more gorgeous every day. You're going to have your work cut out for you."

I stare at him, emotionless, waiting for him to explain.

"It means you're going to have competition."

Possessiveness spreads through my chest. "I don't fucking think so."

"Knox!" Dad scolds me.

"Well, you better treat her right," John chimes in.

"Of course."

I thought I was stating the obvious. The lot of them will castrate me if I hurt her. Anyway, they have nothing to worry about.

I'm not naïve. I see the way women look at me. I'm confident that between my looks and my family's wealth, I wouldn't have to say much to take a woman home with me, but that's just it. I care for no one except Zara. She's my entire world.

A server comes around, offering us some posh food that looks like garbage. I don't know how my mom eats it.

"Where's the sausage rolls or something edible at least?"

Dad laughs. "There will be no sausage rolls tonight, son."

"It's an eighteenth birthday party, not a wedding," I point out.

"Did Zara like the ring?" Dad asks.

I think back to the look of happiness on Zara's face when she saw it. "She sure did."

Dad sighs with a smile. "I knew she would."

The crowd goes quiet. I turn my head toward the entrance. I freeze and swallow hard. Zara always looks good—a classic beauty with creamy skin, a petite build, chocolate-brown eyes, and long black hair. Tonight, she looks older than her age.

When her eyes land on me, her genuine smile hits me right in the chest. She rushes over, so I meet her halfway. She hugs me, with one hand around my back and the other on my chest. I peek at the sparkling ring on her finger.

"You look handsome," she says.

I pull at the collar of the button-up shirt and lean down and lower my voice. "I feel ridiculous." *In this stupid suit Mom made me wear.*

"Well, you don't look it."

My eyes make their leisurely way up her body. "You look incredible." Desire floods me when I look at her lips and feel the need to kiss her.

She blushes. I lean closer and fold my arms around her back. I take a deep breath through my nose. "You smell amazing."

"I'm happy you like the new perfume. It was a present from Iris."

I lean down, nuzzle her neck, and pretend to bite her. She squeals and giggles.

"Have you seen Misty? I want to talk to her about my car. I don't know how she kept it a secret from me. She's terrible at keeping secrets."

I cringe and try my best to keep my face passive. "I'm sure she's around here somewhere."

Her smile fades.

"Don't worry about it." I grab her hand and we walk through the house. There're a few stares, probably because I'm leading the birthday girl away from the party, but I need a moment alone with her.

I slide the back door open. After she walks through it with me, I pull her to me, with one hand behind her back, the other tipping her chin up. My breath quickens at being so close to her.

Leaning down, I bring my forehead to hers. "I love you," I whisper. I might be only eighteen, but I know what love feels like because I couldn't imagine it feeling any better than it does now.

She lets out a gasp, but before she can respond, I bend down and bring my lips to hers, where they belong. Zara's lips are soft, and the kiss is tender at first. My mouth parts hers, my tongue sliding in as a low noise escapes my throat. Our tongues move together, teasing and searching. My body feels overloaded with senses, from her taste to the feel of her small frame against mine. Her arms snake around the back of my neck and she stands on her toes, eagerly deepening the kiss.

Fire burns through me, eager, intense, and full of passion. I pull her closer. Her hands tangle in my hair and she lets out a soft, seductive noise that makes my dick harden. I pull back.

One ragged breath . . . two ragged breaths. I kiss her jaw, then her forehead. I loosen her arms from around my neck and step back.

Someone calls Zara's name from inside the house. My head falls back, my eyes closing.

She frowns and touches her now-plump lips, and it takes everything in me not to take her mouth in mine again.

I let out an exaggerated groan. "We'd better go."

She pauses, so I pull her to my side and place one more lingering kiss on her head. I subtly readjust myself as I open the door.

Zara pauses and peers up at me. "Knox."

"Yes, precious."

"I love you too."

I smile at her, warmth flooding my chest.

We reluctantly walk inside. I stay back and lean against the wall. Zara makes her way around the crowd, thanking family and friends for coming.

Misty walks down the stairs, patting her hair. When she reaches the bottom and sees Zara, she dashes to her. I look up, knowing it won't be long until I see my brother walking down the same stairs. A minute later, he does.

When he sees me, I shake my head at him.

"What?"

"It's Zara's birthday. You couldn't wait?"

"It was your suggestion!"

"I was being sarcastic. The last thing I want is to see Zara upset."

His eyes narrow a fraction. "Why would she get upset?"

"It's a big day for her is all that I'm saying. If she finds out that you two are sleeping together, and she hears it from anyone but Misty, it could upset her, and I wanted her to have a good day."

He groans. "You've made your point. I couldn't resist Misty tonight. Her in that dress." He clicks his tongue.

"I don't want to hear about it. When is Misty going to tell Zara? I hate keeping shit from her."

He pats my back. "Soon, I promise."

"Good!"

Misty and Zara make their way to us.

"We have two hours before cutting the cake, so let's have a few drinks before they notice," Misty points out.

My eyes dart to Zara. "You don't have to drink if you don't want to," I reassure her.

She drops her eyes to the floor and then looks back up. "I want to." She peers back at Misty. "Are you sure you should drink when you're already sick?"

Misty waves her off. "I'm fine. I swear." Then she clasps her hands in excitement. "Taking a ride on the wild side, are we, sister?"

Zara's smile matches hers. "I guess so."

"I can't wait for you to try my favorite whiskey," Misty says.

"You won't regret it, I promise." Misty pauses in thought for a second. "Until tomorrow . . . you will definitely regret it tomorrow."

BEST
FR-ENDS

THREE
TURNING POINT

Zara

Age: Eighteen

Misty groans as she trudges into my bedroom, looking like death. She plops down on the bed beside me.

"Did you have a little too much alcohol last night?" I ask, trying to keep the amusement out of my voice.

She rubs her temples as she closes her eyes. She and Kane had much more than Knox and I did.

"Hmm, don't remind me. My head's about to explode."

I snicker. Always so dramatic.

A thought comes to mind as my eyebrows furrow. "Where did you go last night? You weren't with Mom and Dad when they gave me my birthday present."

That question is a little silly. Misty didn't have to be there.

She stares blankly, taking a moment to respond. "I must have been stuck talking to someone from the family. You know what they're like."

I frown. I didn't see her anywhere in the main room.

"Sorry, I shouldn't have left you."

I force a fake smile. "It's fine."

Misty looks toward the bedroom door. "Do you want to watch a movie in the living room?"

"Sure."

We've binge-watched Netflix for two hours when Knox and Kane walk in. Kane stares at Misty, and when I look at her, she's still pale. Her arms are crossed and she's glaring at Kane.

"Aren't you a ray of sunshine this morning?" Kane says, then chuckles.

"It's your fault I'm this sick. You're a bad influence. Why aren't you hungover?" Misty grumbles.

He sits on the other side of her. "Because I'm not a lightweight!"

She shoves him. "I'm not a lightweight!"

Knox sits on the other side of me and gives me a genuine smile.

"Yeah, you are! What are we watching?" Kane asks.

"Some superhero series," Misty responds.

"Boring!" Kane exclaims.

Misty huffs. "Who cares about the storyline? I'm here to watch those fine men in their tight outfits."

"Of course you are," Kane deadpans. "Me and Knox have put our board shorts on. How about we all go for a swim?"

"Sounds good," I reply.

Kane's face brightens. "We'll meet you at the pool."

I rush up the stairs, but I can't help but look back when I reach the top. Misty's holding on to the rail to help herself up.

From my wardrobe, I pull out the drawer that contains my swimsuits. My fingers travel along the silky material. As I'm looking at them, I admire my ring. It shimmers in the light with the movement of my hand. I can't get over how beautiful it is.

After getting into my swimsuit, I go downstairs and to the kitchen for water, as my mouth is dry from last night. I chug a whole bottle before heading to the linen closet for towels, then make my way to the pool.

When I open the gate, I see Misty lying on a huge inflatable swan in the water, with massive sunglasses covering her eyes. Knox is sitting on the edge of the pool, bopping to the music pumping through the speakers.

My eyes scan his body. I got lucky with him. He has an athletically lean body with a defined chest, broad shoulders, and wavy, messy bed hair. I can see all his muscles with perfect clarity, even from here.

In my peripheral vision, Kane comes flying out and runs toward the pool. He jumps in, folding his body as he hits the water hard, and splashes a wave onto Misty and Knox. Once Kane resurfaces, he laughs at Misty, who is furiously wiping droplets from her sunglasses.

"Real mature," she quips.

He grins at her, showing all his teeth. Kane acts like the youngest, but he's the oldest at nineteen. Misty and Knox are eighteen, and now, so am I.

As if he senses my gaze, Knox looks up and gives me a sexy smile that's reserved only for me. I smile back. If I get to see that smile every day, I'll die a happy woman.

THE NEXT DAY, I WAKE UP TO THE ABRUPT SOUND OF THE ALARM on my phone. Clasping the phone in my hand, I blink from the bright light. We're going to be late for school! Misty threw up again yesterday evening, so we had an early night.

I stumble to my wardrobe and change into skinny jeans and a casual beige shirt. I brush my teeth before I go to see

Misty. My feet pad against the floor on my way to her bedroom. When I open the door, she's curled up in a ball. She brings the comforter down from over her face. Her blond hair is a tangled mess. She has dark circles under her eyes and looks pale.

I rush over and sit on the bed beside her. "I thought you said you were feeling better?"

She shakes her head. I give her a pointed look. "Well . . . if it's not the food and it's not the alcohol, you're going to have to see a doctor."

Her lips curve into a deep frown. "I know."

"Are you going to let me ask Iris to call the family doctor?"

"No, no. I'll do it."

"Do you want me to go get you some breakfast?"

She sits up in bed, massaging her temples. "No. I'll just vomit it up."

Glancing at my watch, I say, "I've got to go."

But I don't want to leave her. Despite my internal struggle, I know Mom won't let me stay home when I'm fine.

"I hope you feel better soon," I say as I walk to the doorway. I turn over my shoulder and blow her a kiss, and I'm rewarded with a chuckle.

I make my way downstairs and go to the kitchen.

Iris smiles. "Good morning. What can I get you for breakfast this morning?"

"Hello, sorry, no time," I reply and lean over the counter and grab an apple from the fruit bowl.

"Where's Misty?"

I cringe. "She still isn't feeling well."

Iris's eyes widen, then something flashes across her face, but it disappears.

"Is Mom home?" I ask.

"She will be out today. Pilates, then lunch at the resort,

and I think she mentioned shopping as well. I would say you'll most likely beat her home. Your father mentioned he was going to be home late from work tonight as well."

"Thanks." I sling the bag over my shoulder and dash out the door.

The limousine is waiting in the driveway. I open the door and slide along the leather seat next to Knox.

"Cutting it fine today. Where's Misty?" Kane asks across from me.

I pull my bag onto my lap and lean over to pull the door shut. "She's still sick."

My stomach churns. I feel terrible leaving her there. Iris will be at home for a few more hours to help her if she needs it, though it does nothing to ease the guilt.

"I'm surprised she hasn't gotten me sick yet," says Kane.

Shrugging, I think the same thing about myself.

The limousine drops me and Knox off at school, then takes Kane to work at the casino. It makes more sense to drop Kane off first, given the casino is closer to their home, but he enjoys seeing Misty every day before school.

The day goes by slowly, and school isn't the same without Misty. I peer down at my phone at all the messages I've sent throughout the day.

Misty

How are you feeling?

Are you okay?

Why aren't you replying?

Knox is in a few of my classes and I have acquaintances, but Misty is my only close friend. I feel lonely and spend the day scolding myself for leaving her alone when she's sick.

At the end of the school day, I call her, but it goes straight to voicemail. Knox and I walk to the limousine.

"Misty's still not answering!" I say with frustration.

"She could have forgotten to charge her phone," he replies.

I press on Kane's name in my contacts and bring the phone to my ear. It rings three times.

"Hey."

"Have you heard from Misty yet?" I ask.

I'm met with silence. Then Kane says, "I haven't. I'd say she's sleeping it off."

She would not be sleeping *all* day.

"Okay, thanks. Bye."

When I get into the limousine, Knox asks, "What's wrong?"

"I feel like crap that I left Misty home alone when she's been so sick lately."

He puts his hand over mine, his thumb rubbing soothing motions on my hand. "Did you end up finding out what's wrong with her?"

"I'm hoping she went to the doctor today. It's unlike her not to reply."

"Try not to stress. The doctor probably gave her some strong meds and she's sleeping."

My foot is tapping the floor when the limousine turns and parks in my driveway.

I lean over and peck Knox on the lips. "I've got to go," I blurt out and shuffle over, opening the door. When my feet land on the ground, I turn to him. "I'll see you tomorrow."

He gives me a small wave.

When I get inside, I throw my bag on the floor, kick off my shoes, and dash through the living room and up the stairs.

When I make it to Misty's bedroom door, my breathing is heavy.

Knock, knock, knock.

No answer.

I'm stuck, unsure of what to do. *Should I knock again, or is she asleep?* I don't want to wake her, but selfishly, I want to know how she's feeling.

My shoulders fall. I should let her sleep longer, but after two hours, I'm checking on her. I drag my feet to my bedroom and put on the TV, hastily flicking through the channels. Time drags on . . . every fifteen minutes feels like one hour. By the time two hours have passed, I stand. *That's it!*

When I reach her door, I bang louder this time. "Time to get up!" I grasp the handle. "You have slept for way too long!" I announce.

I feel silly when she's not in her bed. Strange.

As I scan her bedroom, I can't see her bag or phone. *She might have left to go to the doctor*, I think to myself. But she's been gone for hours now, and she hasn't replied to my texts or my phone call.

I huff. She will hear it from me when I find her. I walk out and search every room before I take my phone out of my jeans and call Kane.

He answers, though there's a lot of background noise.

"Is Misty with you?" I ask him.

"Nope! She sent me a message about coming to see me, but I checked with Mom and she never did. I messaged Misty back, but she never replied. Me and Knox are out for dinner with Dad."

"Well, she's not at home," I reply.

"Is her car there?" Kane asks.

I didn't look, but I presumed it would be in the garage. I move to the stairs, and when I get to the bottom step, I lean toward the wall and flip the light switch.

"No," I reply. "Her car's gone."

"She's out, then."

"No, Kane. She's been gone for hours."

"Can you call Misty's phone?" he asks someone on his end.

I bite my lip, waiting impatiently.

"It went straight to voicemail," Knox says in the background.

My heartbeat quickens as a feeling of dread settles in my stomach. "Something isn't right. She's never ignored my messages all day."

"Maybe she went to the shops," Kane suggests.

"She's sick. You should have seen her this morning. She couldn't get out of bed. So she wouldn't have gone anywhere." I try to keep my voice even, but my chest is tightening and my throat is closing, making it difficult to breathe.

"Don't get ahead of yourself. She's obviously left to go somewhere in her car. If she hasn't shown up by seven, we'll help you search for her, but it's still early. Don't stress—she'll turn up."

He was wrong.

FOUR
THE HEAVY BURDEN OF GUILT

Six weeks later

Knox

Age: Eighteen

ZARA'S HOUSE HAS BEEN INUNDATED WITH PEOPLE. HER PARENTS Helen and John, me, and my mom sit in the dining area, waiting for the psychiatrist to come out after talking to Zara.

I rub my eyes, which burn from staying awake for so long. Zara woke up screaming again, and it takes a while to settle her down to go back to sleep. Then I stay wide awake worrying about her.

I don't know what's going on in the investigation into Misty's disappearance. Mom's been communicating with the police and a private investigator, but no one can find her. I zone in and out of conversations, feeling as though I'm an unwilling participant in this nightmare.

"Knox, how did it go with you and Kane with the posters?" Helen asks.

The posters she gave us has a recent photo of Misty under "Missing person." Below the photo is a detailed description of her looks, height and weight, and the car she drives. It also has the police phone number and a mention of the million-dollar reward my mom has offered in relation to anyone providing details that can locate Misty.

"They are posted in the front window of nearly every business in Crown Village, and Kane and I put them up all over the amusement park." Someone must have seen something.

"Thank you," Helen responds softly. "Did Kane go home?"

"Ah . . . yeah," I answer.

Kane was drinking from his flask while we were handing out and putting up posters. I hate seeing him in pain and watching him self-destruct.

I look around. "Zara asked where Iris went. She noticed she hasn't been around. When will she be back?"

Helen's mouth opens, but Mom speaks. "She finished up with the Pratts. Said she wants to spend more time with her family."

My stomach sinks. I don't want to tell Zara.

"Why didn't Iris say goodbye? Why would she do that to Zara when's she's already hurting?"

Annoyance clings to me. What the hell is wrong with everyone? Misty disappears, Iris leaves without so much as a bye, and I've noticed Mom gradually pulling away. I thought she would be here every day with me to support the Pratts, but she randomly turns up to see them, and it's like her offering a reward is doing "her part."

Helen looks to Mom for an answer, which is weird. "I'm

not too sure. Maybe Iris wanted to give the family some space," Mom answers.

I clench my fist repeatedly as I breathe deeply, trying to calm down, because sometimes everything gets so over-whelming I can't breathe. My life used to be easy, then Misty went missing and everything turned to shit. There's this lingering anger and bitterness toward everyone who has brought pain to Zara.

"Have you given any thought to enlisting yet?" Mom asks, causing my body to freeze.

I glare at her. It's not the right time to talk about this. I considered it before Misty's disappearance because I was never interested in the casino or managing any other busi-ness. That's what Kane wants to do, not me. I want to do something I'm proud of, but I'm not leaving Zara and her family now. They need me.

John frowns but Helen's eyes are wide. "When are you going to do that?" Helen asks.

I shake my head. "I'm not going anywhere." Zara needs me . . . my brother needs me.

"Knox has always wanted to join," Mom adds.

My mouth tightens and my eyes dart to the stairs, checking that Zara isn't around. I've never spoken to Zara about my thoughts of joining the military because it means I would be away from her for long periods over many years. Now I definitely can't go, and I don't want Helen and John thinking I'll desert them and Zara during this. I'm not like everybody else.

"I know you feel like you have to stay for Zara, but you can follow your career in the military if that's what you want. Misty will be back soon, you'll see," Helen says.

I hope she's right, but I would never have thought Misty would leave.

Everyone stops talking as the doctor enters the room. He looks at us and shakes his head. He's frowning. "It's my professional opinion that Zara should seek ongoing treatment. She's experiencing a nervous breakdown, considering all you described." He looks at Zara's parents, then me. "The stress of her sister's disappearance has caused anxiety and depression, which has made her isolate herself here at her home.

"She's not eating or sleeping well or looking after herself. I took a blood test to see, but she may need IV fluid if she isn't drinking any water. I have prescribed her anxiety and antidepressant tablets for the morning and an antipsychotic to help her calm down at night. However, I think it's best Zara goes to a facility where she can get twenty-four-hour care."

The blood drains from my face. John is nodding, whereas Helen has tears in her eyes again.

"Is the stress why Zara has also been losing so much hair?" Helen asks.

I flinch. I noticed that too.

"Yes," the doctor replies.

Mom puts her hand on Helen's arm. "That medical treatment center I was telling you about has the best resources money can buy, and I want that for Zara. I told you I'd pay for it, so you don't have to worry about a thing."

"It's a bit soon to be discussing that, don't you think?" Irritation infuses my tone. "I'm here. I can make sure she takes her tablets."

I look between Helen and John. "Let me help her, please," I beg. No offense to them, but they are struggling as well. I can look after Zara. "What if Misty comes back? Zara won't leave, not now."

I don't mention that she hates when I have to leave her too, even for short periods, but I believe I can be there for her, be what she needs.

Helen bobs her head and peers at me. "It does seem too early, but it's something we can look at if she gets worse."

"These are the prescriptions." The doctor leans over with a piece of paper in his hand. Helen takes it from him. "There are instructions on how much she is to take of each tablet and for how long. You'll see that there is a gradual increase with each medication. If Zara gets worse or has any severe side effects, please call me."

"Thanks," Mom says to the Pratts' family doctor. "I'll pay for any and all of Zara's expenses."

"We can't allow you to do that," John replies sharply.

Mom lifts her chin. "You can, and you will. Let me pay Zara's medical bills. You just focus on your family."

There's no fight in Zara's parents. They look as exhausted as I feel.

After the doctor leaves, Helen turns to my mom and asks, "Has there been any update from the private investigator?"

"None. I have spoken to the local police that are managing the case and who we have in our pockets. One said that because she is over eighteen, Misty legally doesn't have to return home. So unless there's proof that there was an involuntary disappearance, there's not a lot else they can do."

I slam my fist on the table. "That's bullshit!"

Helen jumps, so I soften my tone. "Sorry."

I didn't mean to snap, but we've done more investigation than the police and that so-called investigator have done. It's us who have called businesses and people, put up posters, offered rewards. What have they done? Interviewed people . . . and what? Checked Misty's phone records and laptop to tell us what we already know—that no signs led up to her disappearance?

I stare at Mom. "You tell that private investigator to do better. It's not good enough. I can only imagine how much you're paying him. Six weeks later and there's still no sign of her?"

When I see movement in the corner of my eye, I glance to my left to see Zara. All conversation stops. She pauses at the bottom of the stairs. She's lost a lot of weight in a short time. It's scary.

"Come sit, precious," I say as I wave her over.

I want to include her in conversations around Misty's disappearance. It's important she talks about it.

She hesitantly wanders over. I shuffle the chair back so she can sit on my lap. I wrap my arms around her frail body and pull her to my chest.

"We were just talking about putting more pressure on the private investigator because there needs to be something that leads us to Misty."

"You should consider the fact that she ran away," says Mom, making Zara stiffen in my arms. "She was a free-spirited young woman who liked to break the rules."

"I don't think so, Audrey," Helen replies. "She didn't take any money out of her bank account."

"But your camera shows Misty leaving in her car. She took her wallet with her. She could have been saving up, or maybe she met someone else." Mom shrugs casually, like she didn't just insult Misty.

Zara abruptly stands. "No! She loved Kane. She would never cheat on him."

I sigh and watch Zara storm away and back up the stairs. "I'll go to her," I tell Helen, who has a deep frown on her face.

"Thank you," she whispers.

I rush up the stairs and to Zara's room to see her lying on her stomach with her arms under the pillow on which her head rests.

"Don't listen to my mom," I say as I sit next to her. "She doesn't know Misty like you do."

"There's so many unanswered questions that I'm starting to think I didn't know her at all . . ."

Her voice is without emotion. Her mood changes every day from crying to anger to numbness.

I tuck her hair behind her ear. "You don't believe Misty would have run away, do you?"

"I don't know what to believe anymore. Are you staying tonight?"

"Ah, yeah. Sure."

I can't shake this overwhelming guilt. When I'm with Zara, I feel bad for leaving my brother alone. And when I'm with him, I worry about leaving Zara. I can't be in two places at once.

I think Zara wants me with her because she's worried that I'll abandon her like Misty did, which is why I don't want to go to the military. I don't want her to leave either. We can get through this . . . *together*.

BEST

FIVE
MENTAL TORTURE

One year later

Zara

Age: Nineteen

A buzz echoes throughout the small room.

"Ow!" I whine as the tattoo gun marks the top of my thigh.

Even though I've had some whiskey, it still burns.

"What are you getting again?" Kane slurs before he takes another gulp from his flask.

Today is the first anniversary of Misty's disappearance, so Kane and I have gotten drunk. I'm getting a tattoo to mark the occasion. It's the word *Misty* written in calligraphy, with two small doves raising their wings to fly. Knox watches with his arms crossed over his chest, the same, usual worried look in his eyes.

Once we're home, Knox helps me up the stairs and insists that I wrap up my tattoo with a bandage so it doesn't get wet before I have a shower. Afterwards, I collapse on the bed and shut my eyes.

When I wake up, I need to go to the bathroom. Knox is asleep next to me, with one arm stretched out touching me. He looks so peaceful in his sleep. In contrast to when he's awake and worry lines mark his forehead—all because of me. Sometimes, I feel like my pain is bleeding all over him.

Knox has been staying on and off at my house ever since Misty disappeared. At nineteen, he should be out partying and enjoying life. There's a tightness in my chest about him spending all his time with me. Maybe he'd be better off without me? Maybe death would be preferable to enduring all this pain? I struggle to stop those dark thoughts from polluting my mind.

During the year since Misty disappeared, I've hated the pitying looks from everyone. It makes it so much worse. People ask how I'm doing, but I sense they're being polite—they don't want to know. I put up a facade, telling them I'm fine while my heart is screaming in pain.

I'm struggling to live without Misty. How do I go from one day having this perfect life to drowning in my personal hell the next? No matter how hard I try, I can't claw my way out. Misty's disappearance has created a wound so deep that the pain won't go away.

There are still times when something happens and I go to call her to tell her, and it's those few seconds of peace I revel in—when I think she's with us, when it hasn't registered yet that she's gone. Every time I travel outside of the house, I search for her in the crowds.

My heart aches from missing her, and my mind tortures me with the memories. Her ghost haunts this house. It's not much of a life I'm living, but knowing that Knox—this beautiful human next to me—has walked alongside me on this dark path makes the struggle to hold on worthwhile.

I slowly get up, trying not to wake him. When his hand falls away from my skin, his eyebrows furrow and he reaches out for me. But then he drifts back to sleep, and I tiptoe to my bathroom and close the door.

I don't look at myself in the mirror because I know what will stare back at me in the reflection. After using the toilet and washing my hands, I open the bottom drawer of the bathroom cabinet and move my makeup bag until I see the shiny silver object. Long before I got the tattoo, I had the thought of cutting myself. I haven't been able to stop thinking about it.

I lift the bottom of my nightgown before taking the cling film off my tattoo. I grab a clean washcloth and wet it under the running tap to pat the smeared ink.

Picking up the icy blade, I take a deep breath. A hiss escapes my mouth as the razor pierces my skin. My eyes water as I drag it across. There is now one cut under my tattoo, marking one year.

Weirdly, I feel temporary relief afterward. The tattoo and cut also remind me that the past was real, that she was real.

I'm so deep in thought that I don't hear the door open. When I see Knox's anguish as he sees what I've done, my high is depleted. He walks away and my body is cold. I let out a heavy breath.

He comes back with supplies from the first aid kit. His touch is delicate as he washes and cleans the wound. I watch him in awe as he treats me with care while he covers it with a dressing.

He kisses the bandage and everything lights up. As he stands, I take him in. His gray sweatpants hang low on his hips, accentuating the V of his six-pack abs. I lick my lips as my gaze continues to travel up his fine body to those whiskey-colored eyes.

He grabs my chin in his hand, his eyes boring into mine. "You bleed, I bleed."

The intensity and devotion in his voice makes me shudder. Overwhelmed with emotion, I can't speak, so I nod. He takes my hand and pulls me back to the bed. We lie back down on the crumpled white bedsheets, his arm around me. I rest my head on his chest and I'm immersed by his warmth. Everything fades as I listen to the steady rhythm of his heartbeat.

SIX
SACRIFICE

Knox

Age: Nineteen

IT'S BEEN THE LONGEST YEAR OF MY LIFE. NO ONE HAS FOUND Misty. Not even the police or the private detectives have any leads. My mom offered a million-dollar reward for any information that leads to finding her. There have been calls, but all have led to dead ends.

This nightmare taunts and follows me everywhere I go. I'm stretched so thin, trying my best to be there for Zara and Kane. There's pain wherever I go, and I can't fix anything or help anyone because I can't bring Misty back if I don't know where she's gone.

For so long, I've been through every conversation and every moment leading to her disappearance that would give me any inkling of where she might've gone. Kane has turned into an alcoholic and workaholic, and Zara is mostly in a zombie-like state. She might be with me, but her mind is elsewhere.

I flinch at a loud crash upstairs. Zara! I jump off the sofa and run up the stairs and into her room. The pain and anger on Zara's face physically hurts my chest. An overturned chair lies by the wall, under damaged plaster and the smashed TV.

Her shoulders rise and fall. I slowly step toward her and reach out, but she lashes out and pushes at my chest. I let her. She pushes and slaps repeatedly, but at least she's feeling something and she's showing emotion.

I see Helen by the door, watching her daughter.

"Zara, stop! No more!" Helen wails as tears stream down her face.

"Don't worry, Helen. I'll look after her."

She gives me the smallest nod. Helen has lost a lot of weight. She looks so fragile now. John needs to stop working so much and come home and be here for his family. I think, like my brother, avoidance and keeping busy is their way of dealing with their pain . . . or not dealing with it.

When Helen leaves, Zara screams, "Why isn't Misty home yet?"

A sob comes from outside. Helen must have heard her. I step toward Zara, put my arms around her stiff body, and pull her to my chest. I lean down and whisper in her ear, "It's okay. Let it out."

Instead, her body goes limp. I gently pick her up, as if she were glass that could shatter, and place her on the bed.

She peers up at me with tormented eyes. "Please hold me," she croaks.

As I lie down next to her, she rolls over onto her side. I pull her into me. Tears roll down her cheeks. A catatonic stare has replaced the flash of anger.

Misty's disappearance has created a tsunami effect that's severely affected my family. My mom has moved away. I thought she, more than anyone, would've been here for Helen, but she went to live at one of our holiday houses in the mountains. She said she's giving everyone room and time to grieve. I think she's a coward, so Kane and I have little to do with her anymore except the occasional phone call. We live with our dad full time now.

Once Zara's breathing levels out, I slowly move my arm off her and shuffle to the edge of the bed and stand. I look back at her once more before I drag my feet to her bedroom door and, as quietly as I can, pull it closed behind me.

Dread creeps up from the pit of my stomach as I walk down the stairs. I've separately spoken with each of Zara's parents about Zara's depression. My thoughts go back to my discussion with John.

His eyes were dark underneath, his hair was messy compared to its normal slicked-back look, and his tie hung haphazardly off to one side.

"I'm losing my family, and I don't know what else to do." His body slumped further into the seat at the dining table.

"I want to comfort Helen, I do, but I don't know how when I'm struggling so much myself."

A deep ache took root in my chest. "I know," I replied. "I'm struggling to be there for both Zara and Kane."

He gave me a sad smile. "Audrey suggested Zara is too reliant on you, and I would have to agree with her. It worries me. The treatment facility she showed us sounds promising. It offers a range of health practitioners to help her, and it has world-class therapeutic interventions. I think it could really help Zara cope and give Helen some peace in knowing she is dealing with what she's experiencing."

Zara would be better off moving away and getting the psychological help she needs. I stupidly thought if I loved her and was there for her, she would snap out of her comatose state and live again. But after I saw her cut herself, I knew I wouldn't be enough.

My breathing quickens as I make my way down the stairs

to search for Helen. As I walk through the house, I hear the TV, so I go to the living room.

Helen is sitting in her usual easy chair, with Misty's blanket over her. Her sad eyes peer over the edge of the blanket, and she attempts to give me a smile.

I sit on the sofa. Tension takes over every muscle in my body.

"She cut herself with a razor blade last night." My voice is tortured and raw.

Helen gasps. "My baby is in pain. She needs professional help."

I let out a shaky breath. "I can't lose her," I try to explain, knowing it sounds selfish.

"You will never lose her. She needs to find herself. I don't want her to go either, but the mental health treatment center Audrey proposed sounds like the perfect place for her. I wonder every day if today's going to be the day where her grief is too much and she . . ." Her voice is riddled with pain.

I know how she feels because I've had those thoughts as well. Every time I have to leave her house, I'm a total wreck, worrying if Zara will be okay by herself. Her grief is so heavy it cripples her. I've tried my best to be the person she needs.

But I feel like a fraud. If I were helping her, shouldn't I witness a change in her? I see a spark now and again, like a firefly—a speck of light in the darkness—but then it's gone as quickly as it comes.

"The psychiatrist thinks she's codependent on you and it's hindering her recovery. You have been there for her. I know you love her, Knox, and I can never thank you for being there for her. However, I think we both know she won't willingly leave you. You are going to have to end your relationship with Zara." She pauses. "Do it for her."

Everything I've ever tried to do is for her. I cover my face briefly. The pain of knowing she would be better off without me is like a red-hot poker in my heart, and my chest is on fire, burning me from the inside out.

I look up at her, defeated. "When?"

"The sooner, the better. Audrey has already spoken to the manager at the center. They have a spot available for her."

I can't reply. She wants me to end our relationship today. I'm not ready . . . but then again, I never will be.

"Your mom mentioned your interest in joining the military. If that's what you want to do, you should pursue it. Don't put your life on hold. Zara will get better, and I believe Misty will return."

I realize Mom was right. It's not like I'm helping Zara or Kane by being here. Now's the time to enlist, while Zara can improve. Maybe later we can get back together. Lots of men in the military have wives and kids. Maybe it could work for us too.

Since Misty's disappearance, our relationship didn't stand a chance. Instead, Zara and I are prisoners of war, caught in the crossfire. I'll never forgive myself for hurting her when I break up with her. But she needs help. And even though I've tried, I realize now I'm not enough. Even if it is for Zara's well-being, I'll still hate myself for ending it.

BEST
FRIENDS

SEVEN
GHOST INSIDE MY HEAD

Nine years later
Present

Zara

Age: Twenty-eight

MISTY IS SITTING ON THE SADDLE OF A UNICORN IN FRONT OF ME, laughing as her long blond hair wisps in the breeze. The carousel rotates to the sound of carnival music. It's nighttime, and it's lit up in a galaxy of colors and glass mirrors.

All I see are her beautiful blue eyes shining at me with that infectious smile. I smile back at her because it's impossible not to.

She looks at me with warmth in her eyes. "I miss you," she says, but the music is so loud I can barely hear her.

My brows furrow in confusion, and just when I'm about to reply, the carousel stops and I'm jolted forward.

I peer at where Misty was sitting, but she's no longer there.

"Misty," I call out, but all I hear is silence. Stepping around the unicorns, horses, and carts, I search for her face, but I can't find her anywhere.

My body jerks and I wake up, blinking, trying to see where I am. My eyes adjust to the darkness. The harsh reality hits me: I've been dreaming. I sit up in bed, my shoulders sag, and I lift my legs to my chest as I hug myself while tears stream down my face.

I clasp the chain around my neck and hold on to it. It makes me feel close to her. The best friend charm Misty gave me when we were young is now one of my most cherished possessions.

It won't be long until it's the tenth anniversary of the day she went missing. Every day she's gone hurts, but every year feels like a slice of pain through my heart. She's like a ghost inside my head, and I don't know whether it's a blessing or a curse because I see her face and hear her voice in my dreams.

I don't always dream of Misty. Sometimes I dream of Knox, the boy who consumed my mind, body, and soul. I believe at the time he loved me, as he always showed me how much I meant to him.

One day, he decided to join the military. I gather he didn't want me anymore, and as much as it hurt, I understood. I wasn't the same girl after Misty left, but it did not stop the excruciating pain of his absence. My soul yearns for him, every second of every day.

Occasionally, he doesn't seem so absent, like I could reach out and touch him. It's times like that I worry I might be losing my mind. I believe both were my soul mates, Misty as my sister and best friend, and Knox as my boyfriend. I know I won't find that with anyone else again.

I look at the window beside my bed. I lean forward and move the curtains aside to look at the night sky. It's a full moon and the stars are bright. I wonder what Misty and Knox are doing right now. Do they think of me like I think of them?

When they left, they cut pieces out of my soul. Those pieces have left gaping holes that have never healed. It makes me question whether I meant as much to them as they did to me, since it was so easy for them to leave. Sometimes I feel like I'm stuck inside my own head, with each thought and memory piercing my heart like shards of glass.

AN ALARM WAKES ME FROM MY SLEEP. IT'S TIME TO GO TO WORK at the women's shelter. When I get out of the shower, I look in the mirror. It's as if it's someone else's reflection. Cold brown eyes with dark circles beneath, which contrast with my skin, stare back at me.

I apply makeup before making my way to the kitchen. I shuffle to the fridge and grab an energy drink before I sit at the counter. The can hisses when I open it, and I take a sip, willing the cold, sweet liquid to give me the buzz I need to get through the day.

My phone rings, vibrating in my pocket. I pull the phone out to see a private number calling.

My body tenses as I answer. "Hello."

"Hi, Zara. It's Mae. Just giving you the heads-up. We had nine new people last night."

"Nine," I repeat. The center is well and truly at full capacity.

"Yes, one woman arrived with five children. The youngest is an infant, so the baby will sleep with her. The other is a young mother with two young children."

"What condition are they in?"

"Mostly scared. They're having breakfast now. After they

finish, I'll talk to the women about the resources we have available for them."

"Great," I reply. A beeping indicates another call, so I pull my phone away from my ear to see my mom calling. "I have to go. I have someone trying to call me."

"Okay. Bye."

"Hi, Mom."

"Hi, hon, how are you doing?"

"Good." I cringe at my lie, but Mom doesn't need to worry about me. "How's your trip going?"

"We're home. Hawaii was breathtaking. We loved it so much I think we'll book to go back."

I smile at her enthusiasm. My dad retired two years ago, so my parents have been traveling, making the most of their free time. "Where are you planning to go next?"

"We're staying home for a couple of months."

"Oh, okay."

I have an idea why, but I don't want to talk about it.

She sighs heavily. "I'm holding a vigil for Misty to remind the public about her disappearance, and I'd like for you to be there."

I cough, then gasp for air. I clear my throat because it feels like I'm choking.

"Are you all right?" Mom asks, concerned.

I pat my chest. "I don't know what to say, Mom," I answer honestly. "Misty's anniversary is painful enough, don't you think?" Tears begin to fall.

"Why am I the only one who sees the benefit in this? I'm hurting too, but what if Misty's picture and a reminder of the reward sparks someone's memory?"

"Who else doesn't agree?" I ask curiously.

"Everyone. You know what your father is like. He doesn't like to talk about it. Audrey mentioned that Kane wasn't happy about it. The only person who thought it was a good idea was Iris."

I pause, waiting for Knox's name to be mentioned, but she doesn't say it. I consider whether I should ask her. He was in the military for years, then moved back to our hometown. Now he's in a motorcycle club. He and Mom cross paths occasionally.

I bite my lip but give in. The urge to find out more about him is too tempting. "Have you spoken to Knox?"

"No, not yet. You should give him or Kane a call. Every time I bump into them, they ask me about you."

My heart races at the thought of communicating with Knox. "I don't think that's a good idea." Kane, maybe . . . but there's too much uncertainty with Knox. I couldn't bear to hear he's moved on with someone else.

Mom sighs again. "Please tell me you're coming. Iris is excited to see you."

My chest lightens at the thought of seeing Iris. I miss her. Just another person on the list of people who broke my heart when they left. "When did you see Iris?"

"I didn't. I called her."

"Where are you holding the vigil?" I ask in a tight voice.

"I've spoken to Audrey and Alec about having it at the amusement park."

I suck in a sharp breath. She spoke to Knox's mom and his cousin. I gather she needed their approval to have it at their family's amusement park. The thought of going back there makes my soul crumble and bleed in pain.

"It's on Misty's anniversary date, the—"

I cut her off. "Yes, I'm well aware of the date." I don't mean to sound rude, but that day I could never forget. It's burned inside my brain. "I'm not sure if work will allow me to take it off."

Guilt strikes me first, then shame. We are always busy, but

my boss would allow it. We have people who volunteer, and Mae can take on some of my responsibilities.

"I need you here." Mom's voice is soft, with an undertone of pleading and sadness.

I close my eyes briefly. No matter how much pain I'm going to be in, I can't leave Mom to go through that without me. We should show a united front. It's been around nine years since I've been home. It's about time I faced the past. I'm surrounded by courageous women at the shelter every day.

"I'll make it work. I'll be there."

"Oh, thank God! I'd love for you to come tomorrow."

"That is really short notice." The pitch of my voice rises.

"You never go anywhere. Wouldn't you have leave available? I don't want you to stay one day and leave the next. You haven't been home since you left for the treatment center."

That annoying guilty feeling strikes again. I haven't been home in a long time for good reasons, because that house is full of memories and those memories are a painful reminder of everything I no longer have.

"I can only ask my boss. I'll get back to you when I get a response."

"Hmm . . . maybe you should give me her number? I'll tell her how important it is that you take some leave."

My eyes widen. "No, Mom. I'm not a child anymore."

"You're still my baby!"

"I'll try my absolute best."

"I'm happy to hear that. Ask for at least a week off and let me know when you will be coming so I can make sure your bed has fresh sheets."

I cringe at the thought of being there for one week. "Yes, I will. Bye."

I phone my boss, who gives me today and the rest of the

week off. She understands my circumstances, as I've told her about my past.

Anxiety creeps up on me once my bags are packed, and my heart pounds faster in my chest. My fingers tingle with nervousness. I climb into the car and start the ignition. The engine purrs to life.

I write a quick message to Mom, telling her I'm on my way. Afterward, I flick through my contacts. I can't bring myself to contact Knox, so I find Kane's contact instead. My finger hovers over the call button. I take a second before pressing it.

Kane answers on the second ring. "Oh, look, it's the friend who never called me back."

Wincing, I say, "I'm sorry."

There's nothing else I can say. After I finished up at the treatment center, I stayed in the same city so that I could still attend my appointments with my counselor and specialists. Once that was over, I remained in the city for good, having stopped taking everyone's calls except for Mom and Dad. I shut everyone out. As selfish as it was, I couldn't go back—and I didn't want to. It wouldn't be the same without Misty and Knox.

"Tsk, tsk," Kane counters, lightening the mood.

"Well, I'm on my way to Crown Village now."

"Really?" he asks, raising his voice.

"Yes. Mom wants me there."

"So they're going ahead with the vigil? It's fucking bull-shit. What's the use? Misty's not going to wait ten years to suddenly reappear. If she wanted to return, she would have a long time ago."

I gape at his anger, but I also don't know what to say to him. "I'm leaving now, so I'll get home around seven tonight. Did you want to get together tomorrow?"

"What about Dad's for dinner? Chinese food, like we used to do."

My heart clenches. I've missed all of them so much. "Sounds good," I reply, blinking back tears.

"How long are you staying for?"

"A week. I might stay longer if Mom needs me."

"Six o'clock at Dad's tomorrow. Don't forget because I know where you live." He chuckles at his own joke. "I can't wait to tell Knox!"

Beep, beep, beep . . .

I look at my phone. He hung up on me! Unease ripples through my body. It's been so long. I wonder what Knox looks like. Does he have a partner? Mom never mentioned he had kids. My chest burns with envy at the thought.

Around nine hours later, I arrive at my parents' house and park in the driveway. I sit in my car, frozen in place. The house hasn't changed in the eight years I've been gone. It wasn't a home anymore after she left. It was more like a prison.

A knock on my window startles me. Mom is smiling at me. I step out into her outstretched arms. She has a fluffy pink nightgown on. When I pull back, tears pool in the corners of my eyes.

She pulls me back in for another tight embrace before letting me go. "Thank you for coming. I wouldn't be able to do it without you."

I give her a sad smile.

She peers over at my car. "Your car is still going, I see."

"And going strong!"

"Zara!" I hear Dad call out. I glance over to see him

walking toward us. Mom steps back as Dad gives me a bear hug. "It's good to see you home." I pull back and smile, though from his expression, I'd say that I wasn't very convincing. "You two go ahead. I'll get your bags."

"Are you sure?"

"Yes, I'm not that old."

I follow Mom, but when I take one step inside the house, I close my eyes for a second, gathering the courage to move forward. Mom's footsteps stop, and when I open my eyes, we gaze at each other. Not a word is said because she knows why I'm struggling.

After I regain my composure, I follow her upstairs until I reach my old bedroom. My eyes fixate on my door because I can't bring myself to look at Misty's bedroom. When I open my door, I scan the room. It looks the same as it did when I was living here, but the memories hit me like a slap in the face. All the good ones of Misty seem to be tainted with the pain I felt from her absence.

"How have you lived here without her?" I ask. "All the memories . . ." I shake my head. "I don't know how you've done it."

She glances at me before she stares out the window. "I miss her every day."

"What do you think happened?"

Her shoulders fall. "I've asked myself the same question, and I can never come up with an answer."

"I don't believe she ran away. She was sick. She lost weight. She loved us, and she was happy."

Mom steps toward me, putting a hand on my shoulder. "In my heart I believe she will come back to us."

"You still believe she will come back after ten years?" I ask, my voice brittle.

"I won't accept any other possibility."

Dad walks in and places my suitcase beside my bed. "Did

you pack for a month?" he gasps, struggling to speak, as he shoots my luggage a dirty look.

I bite back a smirk. "Are you okay, Dad?"

He stands taller, rolling back his shoulders. "Yes, I am. We got you your favorite sushi downstairs."

I grin in appreciation.

"We'll let you get settled in," Mom says.

When they leave, I browse the bookshelf to see a photo of Knox, Kane, Misty, and me standing by the pool with our arms around each other, laughing. I sigh at those good times we shared. My fingertips brush the soft material of the satin quilt. My body trembles as I remember how Knox's scent used to linger in the sheets, how he used to hold me. As much as I hate to admit it, *I miss that feeling.*

EIGHT

CRAVING A TASTE

Knox

I'M SITTING AT THE TABLE OUT IN THE BACKYARD WHEN MY PHONE rings. My brother's name stares back at me.

"Yes, Kane?"

"Fuckin' hell . . . where do I even start?"

"Just say it."

I don't want to listen to him carry on. There's no need for bullshit. He needs to be clear from the beginning.

"Zara's coming back home tonight, and she's staying for a whoooollle week."

My body turns to stone. My phone falls onto the table, but I remain paralyzed. I take a moment before I slowly pick up my phone.

"Bro, you there? Knox!"

"I'm here."

"Has Mom called you about the vigil?" he asks.

"I had a few missed calls . . ." I've never been able to forgive her for leaving us.

He lets out a heavy sigh, causing me to frown.

"It's for Misty, isn't it?" I ask.

"Mmm," he answers solemnly.

"I'll be there."

"I'll keep you updated. And Knox?"

"Yeah?"

"We're having dinner tomorrow at Dad's. Six o'clock. And Zara's coming."

My dead black heart beats for the first time in a long time. "I wouldn't miss it."

"I bet," he says with a hint of sarcasm.

"See you then!"

"Is that a smile?"

I look up to see Viper walking toward me with a grin.

"You smiled!" he says, but my eyes narrow. He takes a seat beside me and playfully elbows me. "It's okay," he whispers. "It can be our little secret."

I push him. "Fuck off!"

He laughs. "Ohhh and defensive!" He blinks a few times, then his eyes widen. "It's that chick, isn't it?" He clicks his fingers. "What's her name . . ." He points at me. "Zara!"

I give him a clipped nod. "She's back in Crown Village."

He rubs his hands theatrically, true to form. "When can I meet her? I've been wanting to ever since you told me and Reaper about her."

I curse under my breath. "Look, I don't think you will." She probably won't even want to talk to me.

"You should have gone and seen her years ago when we got back from the military."

"I have seen her," I point out, though I know what he's talking about.

"No, like in person, instead of stalking her."

My lip twitches, though I try my best not to smile. "It's not stalking. I go a few times a year to check up on her. I like to know that she's doing okay."

I have resisted the urge to go to her and talk to her. But she's set up a new life, one without me in it. She doesn't come home because of her grief, and I could never ask her to stay in a place that strongly affects her. She seems a lot better than she was, and her well-being will always be more important than my own.

"Ah, yoo-hoo?"

I blink twice, Viper coming back into view. "Sorry, I was out of it."

"Women do that to ya."

I raise an eyebrow. "And how would you know? Have you even been in a relationship before?" I ask. Axle walks toward us.

Viper snorts. "I'm not stupid!"

Axle sits beside me with a wide smile, looking at Viper. "I strongly disagree."

Viper points to his patch. "I'm smart. See this patch? VP, motherfucker."

"That's because you love sucking Reaper's dick," Axle says, flicking his balled fist to his mouth in a jerking-off motion.

Viper's grin spreads. "You're a bastard!"

Axle laughs and slaps the table.

My lips mash together as I try not to laugh at these idiots.

Axle's jaw drops.

"What?" I ask.

He stands and leans over, touching my forehead with his hand. "Are you feeling okay? Do you need to go to the hospital?"

I shove his hands off of me.

"He's smiling because he finally gets to see his girl," Viper says.

My eyes narrow at Viper's big mouth. Though I would give anything to call her mine.

"What girl?" Axle asks. He clears his throat, giving me a pointed look. "What girl?"

The only one.

All those years watching her from afar, now I can see her, touch her, and—if she can forgive me—be with her again.

AFTER SPARRING WITH VIPER, AXLE, AND RAGE, I'M FRESHLY showered and lying on my bed, thinking about Zara. I lived and breathed her. Who I was pales compared to what I have become. There's no going back because I can't erase the past, but every day away from her felt like I was dying a little each day.

I've missed the feel of Zara's silky hair cascading through my fingers, the scent of her perfume, and the taste of her lips. Everything about her. Each time I saw her, a pang of regret stung my chest, followed by self-loathing. I shouldn't regret putting her well-being above my own feelings, but every day without her has been a struggle.

After she left, my life revolved around the military, and now the MC. I have meaningless sex with escorts to fill the void.

Time may have moved on, but I haven't moved on from her. I can't, and I've never wanted to. Every time I left Zara to come back home to the MC, I consumed myself with work. Being the sergeant at arms is easy because without Zara in my life, I have no heart or any real moral compass. I enjoy hurting others—it's a reprieve from my pain. That's what Demon and I have in common: fucked-up pasts. Demon is the enforcer, my right-hand man that protects patch members and the club.

The smell of cooked food wafts into my room. Reaper's ol' lady, Ava, can cook! I was unsure about her at the beginning, but despite how much pain she's been through with her ex-husband, she still is friendly to everyone. She reminds me of Zara.

I jump off the bed and grab my phone and wallet from the side table. I shove my wallet in my back pocket and swiftly head down the stairs to the kitchen. I inhale deeply, which makes my stomach growl.

I walk past the living room to see Elena, Axle, Viper, Candy, and Twitch watching TV. The echo of loud cracks gives me the impression the other men are outside practicing their shooting.

As I step into the kitchen, I lightly knock on the cupboard, aware of how jumpy Ava can get. But over time, she seems to have gotten more comfortable here. But I still don't want to trigger her.

She looks up at me and smiles.

"Do you know when dinner will be ready?"

"At least an hour. There's a big turkey in the oven."

I give her a chin lift, proceed through the house, and grab the keys to the van. I hope Zara likes the present I'm going to buy for her.

After dinner, there are conversations around the table. I lean in closer to Reaper. "I need to speak to you at some point."

He slowly nods. "I've been meaning to try these new cigars I got. How about we go out the back and talk?"

I rarely have a serious one-on-one conversation with Reaper because my life is the club, so I gather he knows what I've got to say is important to me.

"I'll meet you out there."

My chair squeaks against the wooden floor when I stand. I pick up my plate and go to the kitchen. Elena and the sweet butts are in there cleaning. I use my fork to scrape off a large portion of my food into the container for the dog.

Elena's eyes drop to my plate. "You didn't eat much."

I pause. Despite the awkward silence, I don't tell her why. She plasters on a smile, reaches for my plate, and takes it from me.

I move to the back door and open it, but I'm met with resistance. I shove it harder. The door opens wide. Conan, Ava's dog, stands there. Judging by the drool hanging from his mouth, he must be able to smell the food. The door shuts behind me, and as I'm walking to the table outside, I look over my shoulder. Conan is sitting outside the door, patiently waiting for Ava to feed him.

Shortly after, the back door opens and Reaper walks through, stops at Conan, and shakes his head. "Rottweilers shouldn't be that fat. Is he getting bigger or what?" Reaper asks as he strolls toward me with a box in his hand.

My eyes skim over Conan's gut. "He has put on more weight."

"I keep telling Ava to stop feeding him so much."

I wait until he sits beside me. "I don't think it's just Ava."

His brows furrow. "What do you mean?"

"Everyone feeds the dog, and most people also give him snacks throughout the day. I know because I've sat here and watched."

I like this spot outside. Trees surround us, the air is fresh, and it's quiet. It's relaxing. I hate being confined indoors.

"Are Viper and Rage still taking the dog for runs?"

"Yes, but the dog gets fed all day and at night."

The back door opens again. Ava comes out with a massive container of scraps and places them in Conan's bowl.

"Sit," she says in what is supposed to be a commanding voice, but she's too softly spoken for it to sound like that. "Eat."

"Beautiful, your dog's getting too fat. I think you need to stop feeding him so much."

Ava lifts her gaze to us. She smiles. "No, I think we need to get another dog."

"Another one?" Reaper pipes up. "One is more than enough."

She quirks a brow, then walks back inside.

"She's getting another dog, isn't she?" I ask, my voice tinged with amusement.

"I fucking hope not." He pulls out a cigar and uses a cutter to slice the cap off. After lighting it, he hands it to me.

I bring it to my mouth and draw in, savoring the taste, before blowing out the smoke.

"Zara's back in Crown Village. Her parents are holding a vigil for her sister's ten-year anniversary."

"Has it really been ten years?" he asks, surprised. "I remember you telling us about her."

"Mom had the police on our payroll. She also paid for a private investigator. I will never understand how Misty just vanished."

"But that's it. People don't vanish. So what happened?"

"Misty was home because she was sick. The Pratts' camera shows her leaving the house in her car, but she never returned. She told my brother she would meet him at our mom's house, but she never showed up."

"How was she acting?"

"No difference in behavior apart from being sick. She was the happiest I think I'd ever seen her."

He glances away as if thinking, before looking back at me. "What about social media or bank accounts?"

I draw in the smoke from the cigar and blow it out slowly through my mouth. "No social media accounts were accessed. They went through her laptop but found nothing to suggest she was leaving. No bank accounts were ever accessed, and they never found the car."

Reaper scratches his jaw. "Do you think she left?"

"I'd known her for most of her life, and not once would I have suspected she would leave, but it's either that or a kidnapping. She wasn't a child. She was a grown teenager. We lived in Crown Village. Someone would have seen it. My mom offered a million-dollar reward for any information that would lead to finding Misty. They would have come forward by now."

"You mentioned a vigil? We'll be there for you, no questions asked."

My chest loosens. "Thanks."

"Will they need any help to set up?"

"My brother didn't say much. It's at the amusement park."

He gives me a blank stare. "That's an odd place for a vigil."

"It was Misty's favorite place, so it's more sentimental."

He puts his hand on my shoulder. "Anything you need, brother, just let us know."

The next day, I lie in bed. I didn't sleep well last night. I've been in a daze, going through the motions. I can't get Zara out of my head. All I can think about is she probably hates me, but I hate myself more for lying to her about the real reason I broke up with her. I've lived with regret ever since.

I didn't want to break up with her, but I had pressure from her family to do the right thing by her. I was the only one keeping her here. It came down to her safety and well-being.

Even though I was selfish and wanted to keep her, I knew if something ever happened to her, I'd never forgive myself.

NINE
BURNING WITH DESIRE

Zara

I smile a genuine smile. Going out for breakfast and shopping with Mom was enjoyable. I was happy to get out of the house. Apart from what felt like running into every person in Crown Village, it was great to spend time with Mom. I've missed her quirky comments that make me laugh. It hurt a little when Mom was talking about the vigil with others in the town, but everyone was sympathetic and respectful.

Since moving away, I've grown used to living in the city and keeping to myself, but I love Crown Village's small-town vibe, especially when everyone gathers as a community. I guess I wish it was for a different reason. Rubbing my forehead, I wince. I have a terrible headache that hasn't gone away all day, probably because of seeing the Harts in an hour.

I look in the mirror at the third outfit I've put on. The first was my favorite tight black dress, but I didn't want to look like I was trying to impress Knox. Second was jeans and a casual shirt, but secretly, I wanted to look good to show him what he's been missing all this time. I think the casual black maxi dress is the winner. It still shows off my curves, but it doesn't look like I'm trying too hard.

I lift my best-friends necklace over the top of the dress. My hand goes to the ring Knox gave me. I pull it higher up my finger. "Should I?"

"Should you what?" Mom asks, making me jump. "Oh, sorry, sweetie, I didn't mean to scare you," she says as she walks toward me.

I give her a sad smile. "Should I take the ring off?" I don't want to give him mixed signals, even though I've missed him.

Her eyebrows squish together and she purses her lips. "Why would you do that? Do you want to take it off?"

"No. He might want the ring back, though. It is a family heirloom."

Mom frowns. "No, he won't. That family will still adore you as much as they did back then. That won't change."

I massage my chest as my heart aches.

Mom sits on the bed. "Are you okay?"

I shake my head. "What's Knox like now?" I ask in a small voice.

She looks away, as if thinking about her answer. Her eyes return to me. "He's the same . . . but different . . . He goes by the name Bomber now."

"That doesn't tell me much, Mom. And how did he get that nickname?"

"I don't know how he got it." She pauses. "Knox looks the same but older. His personality . . ." Her hand goes to her chin. "Well, he's harder now. He has more life experience, and he's come back from war, so I understand, but I guess you'll see what I mean when you spend time with him. I've heard a few rumors about their MC, but I could never imagine the Knox I knew to be violent, so I guess that's what they are—

rumors. But then again, he is the sergeant at arms of the club."

I pinch my lips together. "Violent in what way? Sergeant at arms. What does that mean?"

Mom sighs. "Don't listen to me. I think it would be best to talk to him to make up your own mind about him."

I grab my phone from the bed and put it in my bag.

"Have fun," she says with a smile.

I walk the few steps to her, bend down, and peck her cheek. "See you when I get home."

My stomach flutters as I go down the stairs. I step through the front door to see a limousine waiting outside. When he sees me, the driver gets out and stands near the back door. One of the Harts must have organized it.

As I walk to the chauffeur, he greets me with a nod.

"I'm fine, thank you. I'll drive there myself."

"Please, miss, let me drive you. David insisted." He must see my hesitancy because he opens the door for me, giving me a reassuring smile.

I can't say no to David. He was like my second dad.

I sit in the leather seat and place my bag on my lap. The chauffeur closes the door. I glance down and pick at the couple of dots of white cotton on my black dress. As the car accelerates, anxiety causes my heart to skyrocket. I blow out a series of quick breaths to gain control.

Do I look okay? Will he be happy to see me or will he not care? God, I don't think I'm going to cope well if he isn't happy to see me. We had a past together, even if he broke up with me, so that should count for something.

I peer out the window to avoid my escalating thoughts. I grew up in a suburban part of Crown Village, whereas Knox's parents lived closer to the beach. As we descend down the hill, the view of the water is breathtaking. It's windy, so the water looks choppy as the waves crash against the shore.

When we arrive, I could vomit. I look up at the cream-colored house. It hasn't changed a bit since my childhood. I'm regretting my decision to come here. I should have met some place, there're no memories attached.

"Ma'am."

The chauffer's voice lifts me out of my daze. He puts out his hand, and I grab it as I get out of the car on shaky legs. After I step onto the grass, he shuts the door behind me. I turn to the chauffeur. He gives me a small smile, even though he just cut off my exit.

I can do this. It's just dinner. I stand taller with some fake courage, walk to the intercom, and press the button and wait. It beeps, and the click of the door unlocking sounds.

"Zara, come on in." David's cheery voice greets me.

I rush to the front door, and when I'm about to open it, it opens wide, and I'm met by David with outstretched arms.

I'm petrified. I can only stare at him. My heart is beating so fast in my chest it feels like it's going to explode.

He hasn't changed much. His hair is a little grayer now and his beard is longer, but aside from that, he's still the same handsome man I remember. The same whiskey-colored eyes Knox has gaze at me.

A smile that shows all his teeth spreads across his face. "Where's my hug?" he asks as his eyes sparkle with warmth.

I breathe out a harsh breath as tension eases out of my shoulders. I stand there for a second, searching his eyes. There's no resentment or malice from me leaving and never returning, just love. I step to him and wrap my arms around him.

He chuckles and takes me into his embrace while patting my back to soothe me. I can't stop the tears from cascading.

He pulls back, and I reluctantly let go.

"Well, I missed you too," he declares as he kisses my cheek. "Just as beautiful as I remember."

Someone's clearing their throat, and I turn to see Kane waiting for me. "Are you going to cry for me too?" he asks, his voice laced with mischief.

I chuckle at him, wiping away the tears with my hand.

"It's because I'm special, isn't it, sweetheart?" David challenges with a devilish grin.

My eyes skim over Kane. He's tall, like David and Knox, but he's grown up so much. He steps forward, pulling me into him. It's obvious he's put on a lot more muscle since I saw him last.

We break apart, and he looks at me. "It's so good to see you again. You look"—his eyes roam over my face—"well . . ."

I assume he means I look better than the last time he saw me. It's good to see him. I playfully squeeze his bicep. "Look at you, all muscly now."

Flexing, he grins smugly. His fitted shirt stretches across his chest and arms, showing every muscle. He hasn't lost his sense of humor.

My body goes rigid when I lay eyes on Knox. I didn't think he could look hotter, but he has aged ridiculously well. His hair is a few inches longer, as well as his beard. I give him the once-over. He's wearing black jeans and a white shirt that shows off his defined muscles. He looks rugged . . . more masculine.

Knox's gaze travels from my feet to my legs to my breasts, then pauses on my face. I shift on my feet, feeling uncomfortable under his intense gaze.

"Can you two not give each other the sex eyes while I'm right here?" Kane declares.

I snap out of my daydream as Knox curses under his breath.

Knox gives me a small smile, and it warms my soul. "Zara," he says in a deep voice. No hug . . . no nothing.

The warmth I felt from seeing his smile and David and Kane vanishes. All that's left is a cold sensation. I frown.

"Knox," I reply curtly.

The nerve of him. All this time and all those years we spent together, and I don't even get a hug? Did I mean nothing to him?

I will not let him put a damper on my night with David and Kane. "You don't have to be here," I tell him, even though it pains me to say it.

Squinting, Knox tilts his head. "I want to be here."

His voice is firm and confident, but I honestly don't know what to think. I'm annoyed. I shouldn't let him get to me.

"Well . . ." David says, cutting through the awkwardness. He looks at me. "I'm going to order Chinese. Is honey chicken still your favorite?"

"Yes, thank you."

He glances at Kane. "Don't you have a phone call to make?"

My stomach drops. They're going to leave me alone with Knox.

I give Kane my best don't-you-dare-leave-me eyes, but his smile kicks up an extra notch. "Why, yes. Yes, I do."

I shake my head at the liar.

They walk away from us, but David looks over his shoulder. "Play nice."

"After you," Knox says, putting his arm out for me to walk first.

I gaze into his eyes before continuing. This is weird, and I'm suddenly overheating. As I walk through the house and into the living room, I fan my face because I'm flustered.

Nothing has changed. David has the same furniture they had when I was here last. I move toward a familiar family photo on the wall.

I chuckle. "Oh, I remember this photo. You and Kane are so young here."

The photo is of the four of them. David and Audrey in the background and Knox and Kane in the front. The photo is professionally taken. Kane is missing teeth, so he must be around six years old, and his goofy smile makes me laugh. Knox looks so innocent here.

I turn to look back at Knox, who's raking his hand through his thick black hair, wearing a thoughtful expression.

"Do you see much of your mom anymore? Is she still at your old holiday house?"

He shrugs nonchalantly. "I don't have much to do with her. Kane talks to her more than me."

"So you don't see her?" I ask again.

"Once a year, if that. She doesn't like to leave her house."

I raise my eyebrows at the animosity in his voice.

It's strange. Audrey used to be busy and managed so many things in our town, the town her family founded. Then she moved away and stopped having anything to do with anyone.

"What?" he asks.

"So much has changed. I think it's going to take a while to get my head around it all."

He moves to the sofa and sits, so I walk over and sit beside him. He inhales deeply. "You still wear the same perfume."

My face burns. *He remembers.*

"Yes, I do. Mom said you're in a motorcycle gang now." I lean toward him. "Tell me about it."

His eyes narrow. "It's not a gang. It's a motorcycle club."

I cringe, hoping I didn't disrespect him. *Club, not gang, got it.*

"Sorry."

He doesn't speak straight away, so I wait for him.

"A couple of us served together in the military. We wanted

to make a safe place for men who were lost after returning home. I own land here in Crown Village, so we didn't have to fork out money to buy a place. We set up here, and I've been here ever since."

Even though he seems distant, it hurts me to think he was struggling when he returned home.

"You never came to see me."

With as much as I tried, I couldn't take away the disappointment in my voice. It still stings.

A sad smile curves his lips. "You were happier without me."

I raise my hand to my bleeding heart because he just cut me wide open. "How do you know that?"

"I checked up on you."

I scrunch my nose. "I never saw you. When did you do that?"

His face falls, and he looks away before his eyes fixate on me. "When I came back from the military and joined the MC, I checked on you a few times a year."

My eyes bulge. "And not once did you think to come and say hi?" Irritation coats my voice. "What's wrong with you? I thought we would at least be friends after everything we've been through."

There were so many times I would have done anything to have him back with me . . . to hear his voice . . . to feel him.

His lips press together into a straight line, like he wants to talk but doesn't.

"Tell me why!" I demand.

"You were better off without me. You looked healthier, happier. I wasn't going to ruin that."

My mouth opens, but Kane walks toward us, so I remain silent. This is a private conversation between me and Knox.

"So what have you been up to?" I ask Kane as he sits across from us in the easy chair. I sense Knox shuffling closer to me until our bodies touch. I gasp while trying to focus on Kane, but I'm struggling.

His eyes light up. "I still work with Dad at the casino." It's obvious he loves working there.

Knox rests his hand on his leg, though it's so close to mine.

Focus!

"And what happens when David retires?"

Kane smiles widely. "I'll take over management responsibilities and become CEO. I heard from your mom and"—he gives Knox a look with a raised brow—"someone else, that you work in a women's shelter. How's that going?" A tinge of sadness laces his question, even though he smiles when he says it.

I look away as I try to think about using the right words. "It's upsetting but rewarding at the same time."

"After everything you went through, how could you work in a shelter helping people in difficult circumstances all the time? I honestly thought you would do something completely different, like be a teacher or something."

I clear my throat and rub my hand up and down my leg. Knox puts one of his hands over mine. That there is the Knox I remember. My eyes close briefly, but I lift his hand off. I look at him and shake my head. He's had plenty of time to comfort me over the years—hell, to even say hi—and not once did he.

I look back to Kane, whose eyes are darting between me and Knox. "Should I leave and let you two get it on?"

My eyes bulge, and I shake my head rapidly. "No. Stay." Kane raises a brow. "Helping other people helped me, I guess. I found peace in giving women and children a safe place to stay and helping them to get back on their feet."

Kane gulps. Misty's disappearance is the only thing I've ever seen upset Kane, and rightfully so. The torment in his eyes is profound.

"Dinner is on its way," David announces. I watch him as he makes his way to us. He sits on the other easy chair next to Kane. "Wait until you try the Chinese food. They've been here for a year, and the shop is literally up the road. Anyway, what are we talking about?"

A moment of silence swells.

"My job at the women's shelter," I reply, since Kane's mind seems to be elsewhere.

"And how's that going?"

"It's rewarding."

"I always knew you were special. What you do"—he shakes his head, his eyes thoughtful—"is incredible. You should be proud of yourself." He looks at Kane, then at Knox for a little while longer. "Because I know we are."

I raise my head and blink furiously, trying not to cry. "Thank you," I respond, emotion clear in my voice.

"Hell . . . don't cry, precious," says David in a consoling tone.

Ouch! I cringe at the nickname Knox used to call me.

"Don't worry about it. I guess seeing everyone has made me a little emotional."

"How long has it been . . . eight years?"

"Yes, it has been." I glance at Knox.

He is repeatedly flexing his fingers and making fists. He gets up abruptly and walks away. His sudden movement makes David frown. As Knox leaves the room, I track his movements until I can no longer see him. When David turns back, he shuffles forward on the edge of his chair, leaning in toward me with sadness in his eyes.

"Can you do me a favor?"

Oh god. Dread washes over me. "Suuuure."

"Promise me you'll spend some time with Knox while you're home."

My breathing quickens. I nod again, feeling choked up.

My feelings for Knox are a hurricane, swirling around. I don't know what I'm going to feel next.

"I see the way he looks at you. He's never gotten over your relationship ending."

Rubbing my throat, I try to find my words, but it's as if my throat is tightening. "But he broke up with me," I croak.

David sighs heavily and slouches. I glance at Kane to see him shaking his head at his father.

"It's been hard without Knox . . . without all of you," I tell David.

The front door buzzer makes me jump in my seat.

"That must be the Chinese. Why don't you sit in the dining room. And Kane? Why don't you tell Knox that food is here?"

"Certainly," Kane responds.

David leaves the room.

"What was that about?"

Kane's brows lift. "What was what about?"

I narrow my eyes at him. "When you shook your head."

He shrugs. "I'm going to go find Knox."

I reach out to stop Kane. I stand instead. "No, I'll go find him."

I walk through the living room, then survey the hallway.

Knox is leaning against the wall. Where he's standing, he most likely heard our conversation.

"Food is here."

He doesn't even look my way. I walk until I'm standing in front of him, but he still doesn't lay eyes on me. I hesitantly raise my hands and place them on either side of his face. Feeling his rough beard against my hands, I bring his head down to make eye contact. His whiskey-colored eyes search mine. The haunted look in his sends a shiver down my spine.

So many questions filter through my mind. *Why did you leave me? Why didn't you speak to me? Do you still love me?* But the only question I can ask is "What's wrong?" because I hate seeing him so torn.

"I've missed you." His voice is a whisper, but the longing crushes my soul. I suck in a sharp breath. My hands tremble against his face. He tilts his head. "But you know what?" he asks, his voice deep and raspy.

The heat in his eyes makes me drop my hands and step back until my back is against the wall. He follows me, his eyes never leaving mine. He raises his arms on either side of my face, caging me in. I swallow hard as desire swirls inside of me.

His eyes drop to my lips, then he leans in close. I feel his breath against my ear. "I think you've missed me too."

My heart hammers. Need strikes me. When he pulls away from me, I wrap my arms around his neck. I pull him close, and when my lips collide with his, a wave of ecstasy washes over me.

This is no slow kiss; this is years of hunger. His hands drop to my waist, and as he pulls me closer, his fingers dig into my side. My arms tighten around his neck. His tongue sweeps over mine, a throaty moan escaping him. My body feels overloaded with senses, from his taste to the sensation of his hard body against mine. One kiss is bleeding into another as he claims my mouth again and again.

He pulls his head back, breaking the kiss, but then lowers his head. His lips meet my neck, and his open-mouthed kisses blaze a trail to my collarbone. Shivers erupt over my body. His lips meet mine once more. But now he's hungrier and kisses me harder, with a vicious desperation and passion I've never experienced before. I claw at him to get closer. He nips at my lip. My eyes spring open, but the pain's gone in an instant as his tongue travels over it soothingly.

"Dinner's here."

David's voice snaps me out of the moment. Panting, I

stand dazed. My eyes dart away, and I rush out toward the dining room.

As I sit, Kane smiles at me like the Cheshire cat. He knows something went down.

David walks in with two full bags and places them in the middle of the dining table. He opens one bag, takes out containers, and lines them up in the center, then leaves toward the kitchen. Knox sits next to me, but I refuse to look at him, so my eyes skim the table. There's no alcohol—dammit! I try my best to ignore Knox . . . but it's hard when my skin burns from where his lips traveled across it.

"Have a little moment together, did we?" Kane asks, amused.

My eyes flash open, but I mask my feelings before glancing at him and shaking my head.

Kane raises a brow at me in disbelief as David returns with beers and a bottle of wine. Relief takes over my anxiety. When he puts the wine on the table, I stand. I lean over and take a glass of wine from him, giving him a tight smile.

David chuckles. "You should have asked for a drink earlier if you were thirsty. I would have gotten you something."

I awkwardly smile back.

"So, tell me, how was rehab?" asks David.

"I was relieved once I confided in the counsellors and my peers. It made me realize that I wasn't alone in going through a traumatic experience and that what happened wasn't my fault."

With a lively conversation and a couple of glasses of wine, time whizzes by. David and Kane tell stories about their antics and make me laugh. The mood is light. I glance at the time—9:00 p.m.

"I'd better get going," I tell them and grab my bag from the floor.

"I'll take you home," Knox says.

"No need," I counter. "Is the chauffeur still here? He can take me back."

"Please let me take you." Knox's tone is gentler. He's almost begging. "So I know you got home safe."

My eyes soften at his request, and I nod.

"I'll be right back," he says and leaves the room.

Kane, David, and I stand and walk toward the front door. I give them a hug, but when I pull away from David, he pauses and whispers in my ear. "Please see Knox. I'd do anything to see my boy smile again."

He pulls back before I can respond. I give David a tight smile. Knox spending time with me isn't going to make him happy. Though I don't have the heart to tell David that.

We step outside.

"Goodbye," I say.

Knox walks through the entrance, then closes the front door. I shiver from the wind. Knox is holding a sweatshirt in his outstretched hand, and in his other is a helmet.

"Here," he says. "You'll get even colder on my motorcycle."

My eyes widen. Excitement and nervousness rush through me, but I look down at what I'm wearing. "I can't get on the motorcycle in a dress."

His lips mash together like he's concealing a smirk. David's words come back to me. *I'd do anything to see my boy smile again.*

I take the sweatshirt and raise a brow when I inspect it: *War Brothers MC* is written across the back, with a skull-and-guns logo. I pull it over my head anyway. I chuckle when I peek down. It comes to my knees. "I look silly."

"No, you don't."

I gaze up at him to see his eyes drifting up my body, and when his eyes meet mine, they're dark with lust.

I swallow hard and follow him to a black Harley Davidson. It's a beauty. He hands me a helmet. When I pull it over my head, it's a tight fit, and suddenly, I'm hit with jealousy. This is a woman's helmet. How many others have worn it? I know I'm not being fair. I have no reason to be upset.

"Can I have your bag?" he asks.

I pass it to him and he puts it in the saddlebag at the side of his motorcycle. He takes out a helmet and puts it on. He steps toward the motorcycle and swings his leg over it and gets on. He oozes sex appeal and confidence. My hands now fidget in front of me. I can't stop staring.

"Pull your dress up a little and hop on," he says, his voice muffled by his helmet.

I grumble as I do so and bring my leg over the motorcycle. I shuffle into the seat but feel the warmth of his back when I move in close.

"Hold on to me. Lean when I do and keep your feet off the exhaust."

"Okay, I will."

I cling to him, letting go of all thoughts and immersing myself in the present, finding solace and pleasure in the ride.

TEN
AN EMPTY ROOM

Zara

I'M GRINNING FROM EAR TO EAR. THAT WAS AN EXHILARATING ride.

"Did you enjoy it?" he asks, his voice hinting that he already knows the answer.

"Yes, I did."

After pulling the helmet off my head, I attempt to pat my hair down. I put out my hand to pass him the spare helmet, but he shakes his head.

"The helmet is yours. I bought it for you."

I stiffen, mouth agape. "You bought the helmet for me?" I clarify.

"Yes, it's yours."

I touch my throat as I gaze at him. "And how did you know I was going to get on the motorcycle?"

The corner of his mouth curves. "I just hoped you would."

The smile. Maybe . . . just maybe . . . there was truth to what David was saying. He looks sexy on that motorcycle, but I shake my head to get rid of the thoughts. I'm not having my heart broken a second time. With that thought, I turn to leave. The high from riding the motorcycle dissipates with every step.

Heavy footsteps sound behind me. Knox grabs my wrist, but I turn and yank my hand away as if he's burned me.

"What's wrong?" he asks with knitted brows.

"I can't do this . . . with you and me . . . not again."

My head's a mess. I need a break to think clearly. His eyes swirl with a mixture of emotions as he turns and strides back to his motorcycle without so much as a backward glance. I watch as he speeds off. I stand with the helmet in my hand, feeling confused at the way we were acting tonight, both hot and cold.

I sneak inside in a daze, hoping my parents won't hear me come in. I curse myself for what happened tonight. After he had already ripped out my bleeding heart, I cringe at the thought that I threw myself at him . . . but I can't stop the way my body reacts to him. His presence consumes me, wreaking havoc on my senses, making my mind go blank whenever he's around.

Slowly, I drag myself up the stairs, thinking about him. I huff in annoyance. David suggested that Knox still cares for me, but if he did, then why did he let me go?

In bed, I lift the neck of the sweatshirt to my nose and inhale. It smells like him. His cologne, his hard, muscular body against mine, and those sinful whiskey-colored eyes all taunt me in my sleep.

THE NEXT MORNING, I WAKE UP DYING OF THIRST FROM THE alcohol I consumed with David and Kane. I swing my legs over the edge of the bed and pad downstairs to the kitchen to get water. On my way back to my bedroom, I grab what I think is the door handle to my room and open it. The sight that greets me makes me freeze on the spot.

I'm not in my bedroom; I'm in Misty's.

A gut-wrenching scream rips out of my throat. I wrap my arms around myself, holding my chest tight, tears coursing down my face.

Dad bursts into the room, with Mom behind him.

"Call Knox," Mom yells. She stands in front of me and puts her arms around me, pulling me into her. My tears wet her top as I cry. I sob at losing my sister, who I never got to say goodbye to.

My parents talk, but I can't understand what they're saying. All I hear is white noise. Mom ushers me to the bed and I sit.

I glance at Misty's wardrobe and notice most of her clothes are gone.

My chin trembles. "Where are all of her clothes?" I ask, distraught.

"Oh, Zara . . . I'm sorry. I gave some of her clothes away to the local charity."

All the air leaves my lungs. "You gave them away? How could you?"

She looks away from me, and I watch the tears fall from her eyes.

Dad steps toward us, his frown deepening when he sees Mom. "Keep in mind, we were broken for a long time. It wasn't until the last few years that we've done little things like give Misty's clothes away. Looking back, we should have put some aside for you, but you never came home, and we knew if Misty were to return, they are material possessions, which we can replace immediately."

I nod at him but glance away. My jaw clenches. To an

extent, I understand what he's saying, but my heart doesn't care. It still aches for her. I wanted everything to remain where it was, and it pains me to see anything missing.

Mom and Dad step out of the room. I'm grateful, because there's tension between us. The front door slams and heavy footsteps trudge up the stairs. I look up to see Knox walk into the room, taking cautious steps toward me.

"I can't stay here. I thought I could, but . . ." I pause. "Get me out of here," I tell Knox, my voice cracking.

He moves closer to me, his eyes full of sympathy. "Get changed and go get me your bags. We'll leave right away."

Relief surges through me. I return to my room and mindlessly pack everything in my suitcase before doing up the zipper. He grabs the handle and I follow him down the stairs. He says a brief goodbye to my parents and looks back at me.

"I'll be in the truck, waiting," he says and leaves out the front door.

My parents' faces are etched with sadness. Tears still line Mom's red eyes. Even though I think what they did was wrong, I hug my mom, peck her on the cheek, and remind her that I love her, no matter what.

My eyes flick between them. "Thank you for allowing me to stay . . . I just can't stay any longer."

Mom raises her hand and rubs my shoulder. "We understand. I was enjoying you being home. What about your birthday? We can go out for lunch."

Guilt assaults me for leaving them, but I shake my head at Mom.

"You know I don't celebrate it. I'm still going to visit you. What time did you want me at the vigil?"

She sighs. "You should celebrate today. It's still your birthday."

I briefly shake my head at her and wait for her to answer.

"It starts at 7:00 p.m., but I'd appreciate it if you could

come early in case members of the community want to talk to us."

I nod, knowing it's only two days away. "I'll be there, but I'll talk to you before then."

THE JOURNEY WITH KNOX IS SILENT. WE TRAVEL THROUGH Crown Village, then toward the national park. When we meet a dirt road, I turn to him. "Do you have your own house out here?"

He briefly glances at me. "No."

I shift in the seat. "Where will I be staying?"

"With me."

An unsettling feeling twists my gut. "So I don't have my own room?"

"No."

I rub the side of my face. I was in such a rush to leave; I should have followed him in my car or got a hotel.

When we reach a gate, Knox puts in a code and it slowly opens. We travel up the gravel driveway until we reach what I presume is the clubhouse. I'm pleasantly surprised. I was expecting some rundown shack, but it's far from it. It's a modern two-story farmhouse in a mix of wood and stone.

He pulls into a shed and parks beside a van, but it's the line of motorcycles that draws my eyes in. Knox turns off the truck, gets out, and goes toward the back of the truck. I open the door and jump down. Knox meets me at my side with my luggage in his hand.

I follow him past the motorcycles, where there's a man leaning over, working on one. When he sees me, he stands and beams a bright smile.

"Axle, not now." Knox clips out to him before the man

speaks. He's handsome, with brown hair and a short beard. He mockingly zips his mouth shut, but when Knox turns his back, the man whispers, "Hello," when I walk past him.

Because of his friendly and playful attitude, I can't help but smile at him.

I hurry to catch up with Knox, and when we walk inside, a tall, solid man meets us by the front door.

"I need to organize a church meeting," Knox says to him.

The large man's eyes lock on me. He scans my face and puts out his hand. "The name's Reaper."

Odd name. I'm guessing it's an MC thing. I place my hand in his. "Zara."

"I know who you are."

My head turns in Knox's direction, and I lift an eyebrow. I'm curious what exactly he has told him.

His eyes return to Knox. "We can have church now if you want?"

Knox's eyes flick to me and then back to Reaper. "Yeah . . . now."

Reaper pushes the door open. "Axle, church!"

"Coming!" the friendly man calls out.

"Help me find the men. Ava and Elena are inside if you want to introduce them to Zara."

"This way," Knox says to me, and I follow him through the house. "Church," he barks when we pass by the living area. His tone makes me jump.

I sense everyone's eyes on me. I'm used to dealing with a range of people within the community, so I smile and give everyone a small wave. A good-looking man struts toward us with a grin, but Knox stands between us. "Viper. Don't start your shit! It's time for church."

Another strange name.

His friend laughs, his eyes full of mischief. He's got a

manicured beard and short hair on the sides of his head, with longer hair on top.

"Why are you going to church?" I ask them. It didn't do much for me. The one thing I prayed for—I begged for—was to bring Misty home, and that never happened.

Viper bursts out laughing. "It's not that type of church." Knox turns his body toward me, giving me an odd stare.

"Is there another type?" I ask them.

"Club meetings, darl," Viper replies.

Knox's head jerks to Viper, his eyes cold.

Viper steps back with raised hands. "Woah! Warning received."

Warning?

"Ava," Reaper calls out as he walks toward us. When I look at him, he's waving at a woman in the kitchen. She puts down the tea towel and walks out. She's attractive, with long red hair, and a curvy body.

"This is Zara, Bomber's . . ."

"Ol' lady," Knox answers.

Interesting. I'm not sure what that means.

The woman's eyes widen and she gives me a smile. She looks up at the men. "You all go to church," she says, brushing them away with her hand. "Us women will be fine." I don't know what I was expecting, but it wasn't her.

"I'll meet you in there," Knox says. "I'll put Zara's suitcase in my room first."

Knox turns to me. "I won't be long." He studies me, and I give him a sharp nod to reassure him I'll be okay.

As Knox leaves, the woman steps toward me. "My name's Ava. Are you hungry? Would you like some breakfast?"

I cringe. My stomach is still queasy from this morning. I won't be eating for a while. "No, I'm okay."

She stares at me. "Are you sure? It won't be a problem. I'd be happy to get you something."

"I haven't had the best morning, so I'm not hungry, but I appreciate the offer."

She frowns. "You remind me of me when I first came here. It's overwhelming, but most people were kind and welcoming."

I don't miss the *most,* part.

"Would you like a drink, then?"

I could do with a stiff drink. "I don't drink very often, but it's my birthday, so I'll say yes to alcohol."

Her hand covers her mouth. "It's your birthday? What are your plans?"

I shake my head. "Nothing, and please don't go out of your way for me." But I can see the thrill of excitement all over her face.

"But I must. Let me bake you a cake?"

"No, thanks. I don't celebrate my birthday."

"Are you making a cake?" I hear another woman say.

I shift my attention to her; she is petite, with long blond hair. When she notices me, her eyes widen, then narrow. She looks at her friend.

Ava gives her a smile. "This is Zara, Bomber's ol' lady," Ava says.

The woman's face instantly softens. "Hi, I'm Elena"—she tilts her head at her friend—"Ava's sister and Axle's ol' lady."

She's with the friendly man outside . . . Okay, got it. I look from one to the other. "What does ol' lady mean?"

Elena giggles. "Wife or partner."

I flinch. "I am not Knox's ol' lady." We are not together.

Elena looks at her sister, and Ava frowns. There's an awkward, lingering silence.

"Where can I get that drink?" I ask.

"So sorry, I'll get that for you now. Come to the bar," says Ava.

I follow the two women, who whisper between themselves.

"I needed drinks early in my stay too," Ava says in passing as she goes behind the wooden bar. I sit on the stool next to Elena. "What will it be?"

I think of Misty and her favorite drink. "A shot of whiskey, please."

"Coming right up." Ava pulls out a shot glass, and I watch as she fills it.

"Is that Crown Village whiskey?" I ask her, glancing at the familiar white-and-black label.

After pouring the liquor, Ava lifts the bottle upright and tilts her head, looking at the label. "It is. You must know your whiskey."

"No, I know Crown Village whiskey. It was my sister's favorite, and it's owned by Knox's cousin, Lawson."

Ava passes me the shot. As I pick it up, it spills down the glass and onto the bar. I lift it to my mouth and toss the shot down, feeling the burn. After I swallow, I wince.

"Was?" Elena asks. "Does your sister have a new favorite one now?"

Elena's question makes me flinch. "No . . . umm." I rub my throat again, feeling it tighten. "My sister went missing ten years ago," I clarify. "That's why I'm staying here. It was too much at my parents' house where we grew up."

They gasp. "I'm so sorry," Ava says with genuine sadness in her tone.

"We had no idea," Elena says. "I had heard about it, but I never knew it was someone close to Bomber. God, I opened my big mouth. I wish Axle would have told me."

"Knox is a quiet person. I doubt he wanted anyone to know."

Elena looks deep in thought, then her lips curve. She points at me. "You're the reason he smiled. I heard Axle and

Viper talking about it. They mentioned a woman, but now I know it's you."

"Uh, okay."

There goes that smile being mentioned again.

"Can I ask you a question?" Elena asks.

"Okay," I answer reluctantly, unsure where this question will lead.

"Bomber is so umm"—she looks up, then cringes as if considering her choice of words—"reserved, and if you don't mind me saying . . . a little cold. How do you deal with that?"

"I haven't spoken to him in over eight years, so there's not much I can tell you. I have spent little time with him too, but everything about him seems amplified."

Elena leans in closer. "Please, keep going. We know nothing about him."

I clasp my knees tightly together. I don't even know where to start.

"Another shot?" Ava asks.

"Two please."

She gets to work pouring them for me. "I think I had five or six shots my second night here." She places the shots in front of me and leans in. "Just make sure if you have to go to the bathroom, you go back into the right room," she says with a wince.

That makes me smile. "Where did you end up going?"

"I accidentally ended up in Reaper's bedroom. But it worked out for the best, I guess."

Elena raises her brow. "But was it an accident?" Her voice was filled with amusement and suspicion.

Ava's mouth opens wide, her hand on her heart. "It certainly was."

"I don't know about that," Elena says in a mocking tone.

"Knox has already told me I'm sleeping in his room. Is there a spare room?" I ask them.

"Yes, there is for guests," Ava answers.

"Bomber doesn't seem like the type to negotiate," Elena chimes in.

I down one drink and place the glass on the bar, then the next. The burn is ferocious. I swallow a few times to ensure I don't bring it back up.

"He never argued with me," I point out, thinking back to when we were younger. "He had a soft spot for me and was fiercely loyal and caring." *Which only increased after Misty's disappearance.*

"Bomber is protective of the club. If he called you his ol' lady, he's going to be even more protective of you, so I can't see him letting you sleep anywhere but with him. There's plenty of single men here, and without a property patch, anyone can hook up with you."

My stomach drops. "I didn't realize. I guess I am staying with him, then."

I have mixed feelings about that.

"So what do you do?" Ava asks.

"I work in a women and children's shelter."

Ava inhales sharply. A flash of terror widens her eyes. Elena peers at her and frowns.

My eyes dart between the two of them. "Is everything okay?"

Ava's body slouches, tears lining her eyes. I stand and lean over, putting my hand on her arm. "What's wrong?"

"I got out of a DV relationship last year. It was a nightmare."

I gently squeeze her arm, giving her a sad smile. "I can contact my boss and see what resources are available here for you at Crown Village."

"Thank you, but no need. I'm feeling better and I'm healing. It's been a slow process."

"Before I leave, make sure you take my number down, in case you change your mind."

Ava smiles. "There needs to be more people like you in the world. Even though I'm enjoying my chef course, I'd love to do something meaningful like that."

My heart clenches. "From what I recall, there's no shelter here, but there might be one in the surrounding towns. You could call them, see if they need any help."

She stands straighter. "Excellent idea. I'm going to do that."

"Count me in," Elena says.

The women are friendly.

"I'm sure they need all the help they can get."

My gaze goes to the living room.

"Who are the other women, sitting on the couches?"

"Sweet butts," Elena answers. "They cook and help out for a roof over their head and food and . . ." She drops her gaze to the ground, then looks back up at me. "I'd say they are mostly here for the sex, though."

Ouch! Another blade to the heart.

They must see the look on my face because Elena is quick to say, "You have nothing to worry about. Bomber never slept with any of them."

My shoulders fall as the tension dissipates.

Ava asks, "The vigil is in two days, isn't it? Reaper mentioned it."

"That's right."

"Would you like some company, or we can help somehow?"

I smile at their kindness. They don't even know me. "Thank you so much. My mom would appreciate the help. Can I have two more shots, please?"

Ava grabs the two shot glasses and brings them down to the bar, filling them once more.

I'm gulping the last one when I hear a door open, followed by footsteps. I sense his presence. The familiar prick of awareness travels up my arms and makes me shudder. I turn so suddenly to look for him that the chair wobbles. I gasp as two muscular arms come around to steady me.

Knox checks me to ensure I'm okay. I say nothing.

"What happened to her?" Knox asks Ava and Elena, concerned. His voice is tinged with anger.

The women go quiet, and I turn more carefully this time. "I needed a drink."

His posture is rigid. "Can you come upstairs so we can talk?"

"I can do that." I scoot off the chair. My head spins.

His arm comes around my back, and he pulls me to his side. We walk slowly toward the stairs as he helps support my weight.

"Lovely women you've got here."

He doesn't reply. He is solely focused on helping me walk, and he glances at my face every so often. We slowly make our way up the stairs and down the hallway into what I presume is his bedroom, where my suitcase has been placed by the bed.

The room is white, except for one black wall where his enormous bed is against.

Aside from a chest of drawers and a wardrobe, there's nothing in here. Very clinical, with no personal touches other than a large painting above his bed. It has a creamy, textured background. The center of the artwork is an image of a butterfly. It looks so real, as though it could fly out of the painting. Its wings are a stunning shade of blue.

My eyes fall back to his bed and its black comforter and two pillows. I can't help but wonder how many women have stayed here. How many women have had him inside of them? I let out a weighted sigh and step to his bed to sit.

When I look at him, his eyebrows are set in a V. "What's wrong?" he asks.

"Everything's all right." I haven't seen him in years. What he did during that time is none of my business. "Is there something you wanted to talk about?"

"I've spoken to the men, and you can stay here."

"Thank you."

I was unaware he had to ask them. I presumed I could stay, but my body slumps in relief.

He sits beside me and the bed dips. "Happy birthday."

"Thank you. I think Ava wants to organize something. Please reassure her that I don't want to celebrate it."

"I can do that."

I lean down, take my sandals off, then scoot back on the bed to lie down. His pillow smells like him. I clear my throat as emotions threaten to drown me. I feel his eyes on me. I peek up to see him watching me.

Knox takes out his gun, which surprises me, though I guess I should have known he would be armed being in an MC. He places it on the nightstand. His belt and holster are next. He lies beside me, on his side.

"What's sergeant at arms mean?" I ask.

"I'm responsible for the safety and security of the club."

"Okay . . . well, why is your nickname Bomber?"

"Everyone has road names. I was in the military with Reaper and Viper. My specialty was disarming live explosives."

Shock and disbelief widen my eyes. I bite down, my jaw clenching. "After everything we've all been through . . ." I shake my head in disappointment. "You'd risk your life? Make us go through that pain all over again?" My voice cracks as tears fall. I roll over onto my side, turning my back to him.

He shuffles in closer until I feel his body flush against

mine, and his arm comes over me. His warmth consumes me. I allow him to hold me, even though he is the one who upset me.

"Every person in my life who I was close to was suffering. I joined the military because I wanted to do something worthwhile, so I could be proud of something in my life because I felt like I was a failure from not being able to help you or Kane.

"When I came home during my vacation, I spied on you and saw you doing better . . . much better without me. Kane wasn't drinking as much either. He put all his energy into helping Dad with the casino. I thought it wouldn't matter as much if I did specialize in something dangerous. I wasn't going to have much of an impact if I died compared to someone else with a big family or a wife and children."

I turn in his arms and a sob breaks through. Tears flood my face. "How could you?" Pain echoes in my voice. "I wouldn't survive losing you too . . ."

He leans over and places a lingering tender kiss on my temple. "Shh . . . I'm still here with you."

After my tears dry, I speak. "It's been hard without you and Misty."

He squeezes me tighter. "It's been hard without you too."

His voice throbs with emotion.

"I still listen to Misty's voicemail. I taped it. What I would give to hear her laugh again or listen to her being feisty with Kane."

There's a brief silence before he speaks.

"I tried . . . My mom had a private investigator. Kane and I called every place we could think of that Misty visited."

I release my breath. "I know . . . everyone tried."

He nuzzles his nose into my hair and into my neck. My eyes get heavy, and I drift off.

I wake up, blinking in a dark room, to see my phone ringing. Knox's arm is still firmly around me. I stretch over to the side table, grasp the device, look at the screen, and bring it to my ear.

"Hello."

"Hey, I was calling to check up on you. How are you feeling?"

"I'm okay. Sorry, Mom, I didn't mean to upset you. I wish I could have stayed with you and Dad, but it all became too much."

"We understand. There's no need for an apology. How have you settled in there?"

"The club said I could stay for as long as I need to. I've met some women here, and they've been warm and welcoming. They offered to help at the vigil as well."

She sniffles through the phone. "That's so very kind of them, and it's a relief that you are okay with staying there. I wasn't sure how you would do, but they sound like a good bunch of people."

"They are. What time did you want me at the vigil again?"

"I'd like you to be there an hour early to ensure everything is prepared."

I pause. "I'll meet you there at six, then."

"Great. Well, I'll let you go. If you need anything, I'm a phone call away."

"Thanks, Mom. Bye."

"How's your mom?" Knox asks, his voice thick with sleep.

"I think she was worried about me." I grab his arm and place it on him so I can sit up and shuffle my back against the wall.

He abruptly sits up, then puts his legs over the bed, turning his back to me.

It stings, but it's for the best. There's so much going on, I can't handle any more.

Someone knocks on the door.

"Dinner is ready," Ava says.

My stomach grumbles.

"Thank you," I call out.

I move toward Knox, put my feet over the edge of the bed, and stand. "Are you coming down?"

He stands beside me, his face emotionless. He puts his arm out, signaling for me to walk out. We move down the hallway and then the stairs. Knox is close behind me. All the members of the MC and the women are sitting at a gigantic wooden table, with Reaper at the head of it.

As I move toward them, Knox is by my side. "Sit beside Elena."

There are two spare seats between Ava and Elena, so I stride to them. Knox pulls out my chair and I sit, and he sits beside me. I glance at Ava, then Elena, and they smile back at me.

After looking at my empty plate, I look at the tacos, large plates with ground beef, and bowls with slices of tomato, lettuce, and avocado on the table. Smaller bowls hold shredded cheese and sour cream. Everyone is helping themselves, so I stand, lean over, and pick up two taco shells, then sit after filling them.

I feel Knox's eyes on me every so often. When I finish, I grab a napkin and wipe my face, then glance at Knox. He stares back but says nothing.

"Would you like me to introduce Zara to everyone?" Reaper asks Knox.

Knox's eyes don't leave mine. "Are you okay with that?"

"Yes. I'd like to meet your friends."

Reaper's gaze returns to the table. "Excuse me." His deep, loud voice carries over the table, and all conversations stop. "I'd like to introduce Zara to everyone."

I lean forward to see everyone's faces. "Well, you know Ava and Elena. Then beside Elena is Axle, who is the road captain." Axle gives me one of his playful smiles.

"Beside Axle is Demon, the enforcer, then Cash, the treasurer."

Demon is covered in tattoos that peek out of his shirt, with both arms and his neck covered.

"Hey," Cash replies. He has short black hair and is leaning back in his seat in a laid-back manner.

"Then it's Rage, a patched member." The youngest man gives me a sincere smile.

"Twitch is head of IT security." The man has wavy brown hair, an ear piercing, and a sprinkle of stubble. He gives me a small wave.

"And Viper is our VP." Viper tips his head, then winks at me.

When I glance back at Bomber, he's glowering at Viper.

I look around the table once more. "Thank you for allowing me to stay in your home"—my eyes land on Ava—"and for your hospitality."

She blushes. "You're welcome."

After dinner, the conversation flows effortlessly. I listen intently to the people around me. Ava and Elena stand and grab other people's plates, piling them on top of theirs, and walk toward the kitchen.

They come back and Elena grabs mine.

"Would you like any help?" I offer.

"No, you stay seated. It's your birthday."

I watch as they and the other women collect everyone's plates and leftover food.

They then bring out bowls and spoons. I wonder if I can fit

in the dessert, but I guess it depends on what it is. Ava walks out with a big smile and a gigantic cake on a tray with one pink candle. As she walks to me, my chest warms and I blink back tears.

The cake is white, with icing swirls around the top edges and multicolored sprinkles on top. I lean to the side, allowing space so that Ava can place the cake in front of me. "You didn't have to do this."

"I wanted to," she says through a smile.

After the women sit, Ava sings happy birthday, and everyone joins in. I stare at the cake, and once everyone finishes singing, I blow out the candle, then close my eyes.

I wish to find out what happened to Misty.

BEST

ELEVEN

EMOTIONAL ROLLER COASTER

Zara

After dessert, I decide to have an early night. Knox leads, and I follow him into his room. There's an awkward tension between us. I kneel, open the zipper of my suitcase, and flip the lid open. I move my clothes aside until I uncover my silk summer pajamas, which are a set of singlet and shorts. I cringe, wishing I had packed something that covers more skin.

I stand and turn to him. "Where can I get changed?"

His face is emotionless. "In here." He turns his back to me, giving me privacy.

I grab my dress, lift it over my head, and throw it on my suitcase, followed by my bra. Then I slip on the singlet and step into the small shorts.

"I'm finished."

He turns, and his eyes drag the length of my body. When I look down, my nipples are erect against the silk material. I cross my arms. His gaze lowers and lingers. When I look down, I see that he's staring at the scars on my thigh. He frowns, so I hastily step to the bed, fold the comforter down, and shuffle under the covers.

The nine marks underneath my tattoo represent so much. They're a reminder of each year I've been robbed of seeing my best friend.

Knox walks toward a wardrobe, opens it, and grabs another War Brothers MC sweatshirt off the coat hanger before throwing it on the end of the bed. "If you're going to wear *only* that"—his eyes dart to my chest—"you're not leaving this room without my sweatshirt on."

I press my lips in a firm line, trying not to smile at his overprotectiveness.

He lifts a brow. "Are you going to answer me?"

"Yes, I'll wear the sweatshirt when I leave the room."

His shoulders fall an inch. He puts his gun into another holster on the side table. He lifts the fitted shirt over his head, and I bite down on my lip. My eyes wander over his muscles, but when I notice the scars that litter his body, my heart feels heavy that he was injured. I look away, not wanting to draw attention to them or make him feel uncomfortable—though, even with the scars, he's gorgeous. They align with his now hardened personality. He radiates masculinity, and all I want to do is go over every mark on him. We wear scars of painful pasts, but it's the internal ones nobody sees that hurt the most.

He steps to the other side of the bed and gets in beside me. I'm lucky the bed is large enough so that we have space between us. As much as I want him, my heart can't handle being cracked open again.

I roll over onto my side to look at him. "Can you ask if Kane will meet us earlier at the amusement park?"

"What time?"

"About five. Because I haven't been back in so long, it

would be nice to spend some time together with just us. I thought going on the rides and eating the food we used to would be a positive way to spend the afternoon because the vigil will be . . ."

Something passes between us. He nods, like he understands without me having to explain how hard the vigil will be.

"Kane will like that." He pauses. "He may joke around and not show it, but he's very much still in pain."

A heavy weight engulfs my body. "Since I've been gone, have you found out anything else about her case?"

"No." A bite seeps through his tone.

"Do you think she left or . . ." I can't bring myself to say the other option.

He looks away, deep in thought. "I can't answer that because, when looking at the facts, nothing makes sense."

I was in denial for a long time. I wasn't interested in the facts because I was in too much pain, and all I cared about was when and if she was going to return.

"Do you remember what happened to her real birth parents?"

"The police interviewed them. They didn't know where she was living, and they had a strong alibi. Everyone else was interviewed and cleared."

What else . . . What am I missing?

"What about her phone?"

"The police wouldn't share the information, but Mom has police officers on her payroll, and she said they told her it showed up nothing."

Frustration builds up inside of me. "What about Iris? Have you seen her around? Mom said she's going to be at the vigil."

He shakes his head. "No."

Even with everything, there's a sliver of hope inside of me

to find something out about Misty's disappearance while I'm home.

"I want to have a chat with Iris—since she was the last one to see Misty. Hopefully, Mom can give me Iris's phone number."

"I'm going to be looking into Misty's case as well," says Knox with a determined look in his eyes.

We are desperate for answers . . . clinging to finding even a snippet of information that we don't already know.

"Can I ask you a question?"

"Yeah, okay . . ." he replies slowly.

"What are your scars from?" There's no judgment, just sadness.

"It's shrapnel wounds from a bomb that exploded."

I nod and swallow thickly. I turn and roll over before I do something stupid like touch him or kiss him. "Good night," I say as I shuffle toward the edge of the bed.

A SLOW, SLEEPY SMILE SPREADS ACROSS MY FACE AS KNOX PLAYS with my hair. I press my lips together, trying not to moan. I sit up next to him and let my eyes travel down his body. Even though my lids are heavy with sleep, my gaze remains on his scars. I reach out and touch his muscular shoulder. His skin's warm as I trace a round, silky scar.

His eyes are closed, and his breaths quicken as my fingers travel from the scar on his shoulder and make their way over the hard planes of his chest. His body shudders as I move down to the top of his abs, where I trace a jagged scar.

My fingernails dig in as they graze over each ab until they reach a light trail of hair that starts from his belly button. I follow it further down to his boxer shorts. When my fingers creep in at the top, stretching the material, he grabs my wrist and stares at me intently.

"Are you sure you want this?"

I blink a few times, then whip my hand away and shuffle backward until my back meets the headboard. "I'm sorry."

Even in my sleepy state, I crave him. His deep frown slices my heart. My cheeks heat as my stomach sinks.

"I'm sorry," I repeat.

He bows his head, then stands and opens the wardrobe. He grabs a pair of dark-blue denim jeans and a white shirt and walks out of the room. I'm left sitting there, rubbing my chest where it aches. I hate seeing the anguish on his face, the tension in his body. I'm doing exactly what I used to do. I'm hurting him *again* just by being here.

I'm being pulled in two directions, one part lust, the other wariness. I want him to hold me . . . The other part of me is terrified that I'm opening myself up to heartbreak, and I can't go back to that dark place . . . not again. There's a light knock on the door, so I hastily wipe my eyes, then pull the comforter up to my shoulders. "Come in."

No one comes in, but I hear a soft voice. "I don't want to intrude. I wanted to let you know breakfast is ready."

A small smile touches my lips. "Thank you, Ava."

"It's pancakes." Her voice brightens, like she's trying to convince me with food to come down.

I sigh, knowing Knox will have a meltdown if I wear my pajamas. I shuffle toward the edge, then stand and slide into Knox's sweatshirt. I go to the door and open it. Ava smiles at me and claps twice.

"Where are you going?" Knox's voice carries through the hallway, startling Ava and me.

I turn to him and narrow my eyes. He never used to be this abrupt.

"I'm going downstairs for breakfast."

"I'll come down with you."

Shifting back to Ava, I say, "Sorry."

She tries to smile at me, but it looks forced. "It's okay. Breakfast is outside this morning."

When she leaves, I stare at Knox, and my eyes trail over him. His fitted white shirt shows off his broad shoulders and defined chest. I lick my dry lips. As he breezes past me, I'm hit with his cologne. A fresh, clean, masculine cedarwood scent. When he comes out of his room, he has his leather motorcycle vest on.

My hands move on their own accord to his vest, and I feel the leather texture between my fingers. "What's this called?"

"A cut."

My fingers rise to the top patch. "One percent, what does that mean?"

"Outlaws."

I drop my hand as a breath rushes from my mouth. He doesn't want to talk to me but doesn't want me out of his sight either.

"I'm going to breakfast," I say curtly.

He says nothing but follows me. I go down the stairs. The music is pumping, and when I hear the vocals of the song, I know it's Linkin Park.

I trail through the house. As I open the back door, people are seated around a large table. Cash and Demon are leaning against the back of the house, smoking.

Viper yells out the lyrics of the chorus, while a very large rottweiler howls.

"Even the dog is telling you to shut up," Reaper says.

There's an array of deep chuckles.

Viper stops singing and laughs. "He's singing *with* me." He bends down and grabs either side of the dog's face. "Aren't you?"

Ava turns to Reaper. "Honey, we have been through this. His name is Conan."

The dog sneezes on Viper. "Really, Conan?" He wipes his face.

I laugh at them, then all eyes land on us, so I give everyone a warm smile. When I get to the table, Ava stands. "You stay seated and finish your breakfast," I tell her while looking from her eyes to her plate.

She has one and a half pancakes left. Her lips press together, like she wants to disagree with me but doesn't say it. She's too kind.

Rage stands. "Here, you can take my seat."

"Thanks, Rage," Knox answers before I can.

Rage lifts his legs over the wooden seats.

"Oh, look at you, Mr. Gentleman," Axle says in a mocking tone.

Rage gives him the finger. Axle laughs.

Elena clears her throat. She waits, then shakes Axle's shoulder. He looks at her. "What?"

She gives Knox a pointed look, then peers back at him.

He shrugs, his head tilting. "What? Speak, woman!"

Elena lets out a long groan. "Can you move so Bomber can sit next to Zara and they can have their breakfast?"

"Ohhh," he glances at us, then stands and moves aside.

Once we reach the table, I sit, but before Knox can, Axle grasps his arm. "I kept the seat nice and warm for you," he says with a cheeky wink at the end.

Knox shakes his head at him.

"Be happy, man. Your woman is here," Axle says with a smile.

An awkward tension fills the air. Elena whacks her forehead with her palm.

Axle's eyes dart between everyone. "Well . . ." He scratches the back of his neck.

"Don't worry about it." My tone is soft. I make eye contact with Axle, and he blows out a gush of air. I don't want to make anyone feel uncomfortable when I'm the one staying in their home.

When Knox sits, his eyes latch onto mine, then they wander around my face. I give him a reassuring smile.

"There are chocolate pancakes on the first plate, blueberry and vanilla on the second plate, and banana on the third," Ava says.

"Ava's pancakes are the bomb!" Twitch says from across the table.

I grab a banana pancake, place it on my plate, and pick up the honey, drizzling it on top.

When I'm finished eating, I leave my fork and knife next to my plate. Hands come out, and it's Knox placing another pancake on my plate.

I shake my head. "No, no."

His jaw ticks. "Please." His voice is rough, but his brows are furrowed. He leans in close to me. "You need to eat."

My shoulders fall. "One more. That's it."

The tension drains from his face.

"Did you say please?" Viper asks. "I bet that tasted like acid coming from your mouth."

Knox tsks back at him.

Once finished, I stand to help the women. Knox stands with me. "I'm helping them take the cutlery and plates inside," I tell him. Viper gets up and steps to Knox, grabs his shoulders, and pushes him until he is seated.

"Thank you," I whisper to Viper.

Viper shakes Knox's shoulders again. "You need to loosen up."

I feel Knox's eyes on me as I make my way to the back door. Cash moves, opening it for me, as my hands are full. "Thanks," I mutter.

"You need some weed to chill the fuck out," says Demon.

Knox never touched drugs when I was with him, but that very well could have changed. I don't dare look back but go inside and to the kitchen. A young woman with blond hair makes her way to me with a wide smile. "Hi, I'm Candy."

I smile back. "I'm Zara. Nice to meet you."

She fidgets. "I can't believe Bomber has an ol' lady. So many women over the years have tried to hook up with him." I flinch. "He always said no, so you must be special."

"I, ahh . . ." I don't know what to say to that, so I plaster on another smile.

"Just, so you know . . . I'm with Viper."

"No, you're not," another woman calls out, then approaches us. Her shiny lips mash together.

"I nearly am," Candy responds, confidence evident in her voice.

The woman's head falls back as she laughs. Then she peers at me. "My name's Mercedez."

She's petite, like Candy, but with brown hair and a full face of glamorous makeup on.

"Hi, nice to meet you too."

Mercedez pivots on the spot and points. "That's Trixie." The woman's hands are in the sink, but she looks my way and gives me a small smile. Trixie is wearing a blue tank top that showcases the sleeve of tattoos on her left arm. She has denim short shorts on, and she has long black hair that hangs down her back.

"And that's Dolly." A smile stretches across the young woman's face. She walks to me and wraps her arms around me, so I hug her back. She's wearing a similar shirt and shorts as Trixie but has short light-pink hair in two pigtails.

"I'm bi," she says with a wicked glint in her eyes.

I chuckle. "Sorry, I'm straight." I have no judgment, it's just that I'm one hundred percent straight.

Her face scrunches. "Dang it!" She playfully bangs her hand.

"Do you need any help in here?" I ask.

"No, we're good," Trixie replies.

Elena puts the sauces in the pantry, and Ava adds more plates, knives, and forks to the pile.

I sit at the kitchen island. Axle comes out, walks toward Elena, and gives her a kiss on the cheek. "Babe, you need to communicate with me. As much as you wish I could . . . I can't read your mind."

"Babe"—she uses the same tone of voice as he did—"I don't know how many subtle hints I can give you. Maybe it's *you* who needs to learn facial expressions and body language cues."

Axle pauses and looks up, as if thinking about her comment. "Nah . . . You know I'm shit at that, so *you* will just have to tell me."

Elena subtly rolls her eyes.

Axle's eyes narrow a fraction at her. "I saw that," he says playfully. When he sees me, he steps closer. "Bomber's real intense with you."

Viper walks through the door, takes one look at us, and struts over. Elena moves closer to us as well. "Yes, he's full on . . ." Elena adds. "I had an inkling he would be protective, but he has taken it to the next level."

My body warms and I blush. "It's Knox. He's always been overprotective. He means well, though."

Axle briefly peers down. "Oh, no, it's more than that . . . He's wound up so tight over you."

"What do you mean?" I ask Axle.

"We've seen him riled up before, but with you . . ." Viper lets out a whistle then leans forward, places his hand on mine, and lowers his voice. "All I'm saying is tread carefully," he says.

"What . . . the . . . fuck . . ." A deep voice comes from the doorway.

I sit up straighter in my chair, my eyes dart to Knox. There's weight of tension in the air. A muscle tics along Knox's jawline as he glares at Viper's hand resting on mine.

Viper is the only one who isn't fazed by Knox's reaction. He lifts his hand with an easygoing expression. "We were just talking," he says in a calm but firm voice.

Viper leans into Knox, who has turned to stone, and whispers in his ear. Whatever he said seemed to work, as Viper pats him on the back and walks away. Knox's shoulders fall, his expression softening.

I walk to Knox and take his hand in mine. I tug him through the living room and out the front door, onto the porch. "Why are you so upset?"

"I don't want anyone touching you."

I can understand how that may have come across with his friend's hand over mine and the closeness between us as he leaned in to warn me about Knox, but it's not like Knox has seemed interested.

"You don't want to talk to me . . . touch me . . . if I mean so little to you, why—"

His lips are on mine, silencing me. They are soft and greedy. His tongue taking advantage, delving in deep and aggressively. I still at first, then wrap my arms around his neck, kissing him back, jerking him closer. My heart beats too fast. A moan escapes me in pure desperation. The kiss heightens sensual parts of me.

He demands possession with every sweep and twist of his tongue. His fingers dig into my hips. His other hand is on the side of my neck as his thumb caresses my throat. I raise my hand and run my fingers through his hair, then begin tugging, which grants me a drawn-out groan.

His hands wander, then squeeze my ass. A shiver travels

down my spine as I feel the rigid outline of his cock through his jeans. He swivels his hips into mine, slowly dragging it across my clit, which makes the ache turn into throbbing between my legs.

The passionate kiss lingers on. Both of us are scared of ending it. He sucks on my bottom lip before pulling away, and every inch of my body hurts without his lips on mine.

His gaze is heavy lidded. He cups my face with one hand. "I will always want to touch you," he says as he squeezes my behind with his other hand. "Kiss you." He leans in, pressing a hard kiss on my lips before pulling away. "Zara . . ." he says in a breathy plea. "You are my fucking air . . . I'm dead without you."

BEST
FRIENDS

TWELVE
BATTLE SCARS

PEERING OUT THE WINDOW, I SEE THE SUN'S COMING UP. I'VE been awake most of the night, frozen in Knox's bed. I'm my own worst enemy—I get stuck in my mind, dwelling on memories of Misty. It eats me alive to know I still have no answers.

It's ten years today since Misty's disappearance, and no matter how busy I am or what I'm doing on her anniversary, I can't get away from the darkness that torments me. Some days, it feels like yesterday that she was here. Others feel like a lifetime ago.

I pull out my phone and go to Misty's name in my contacts and press on the message icon. I slide my finger up, looking at the unread texts I've written to her over the years. I start typing.

Misty

> Hey bestie, Ten years since you've been gone, and it pains me to not see you. I miss your jokes and the way you made me laugh all the time. Every day you made me smile, and at the time I didn't realize how lucky I was to have you in my life. I wish you could see the work I've done at the shelter. I think you would be proud. Mom and Dad are happier now that Dad retired. I didn't think they would ever recover from not having you in their lives, but they are, like the rest of us. We are slowly learning, over the years, how to live our lives without you in it. I think I'm finally coming to the realization that, for whatever reason, you're not going to return to us. I just wish I knew why. I'm back in Crown Village to help with your vigil, though the hope of you returning is small. Mom's never given up. It's days like today that I miss your advice about how to handle Knox. As much as he tore my heart out, I still love him, but after everything, I don't think I could handle another heartbreak. I'm trying to keep my distance, but so far, I'm failing miserably. Wherever you are, please know that I'll never forget the friendship we shared, and no matter how much time passes, you're always in my mind and in my heart. *Best friends forever, Zara xxx*

Tears stream down my face. I give myself permission on this day to feel everything—the loss, the pain, the darkness but also the light of her memories. Slowly sitting up, I inch to the side of the bed, place my feet on the ground, and tread to my suitcase, where I take out my toiletry bag. I make my way to the door and open it. The slight creak of the door makes me curse. I look back to see Knox still asleep.

I walk into the bathroom, then lock it behind me. I zip open the toiletry bag and pick up the sharp object with my fingers. My throat tightens when I look down at the top of my thigh where Misty's tattoo is, along with nine neat scars underneath.

Her anniversary is the most painful and intense. The scars are punishment and reprieve. I wish I could find out what happened. I need answers so I can find peace.

My hands move to the silk-like scars on my leg and hover just below them. I rest my foot on the bathtub and lift my pajama shorts. Taking a deep breath, I push the blade into my skin, wincing at the sharp, piercing pain. I drag the blade in line with the other scars and watch the blood trickle down my leg, leaving crimson drops on the floor.

On the most painful day of the year, the cutting helps with the pain in my chest. Tension releases, almost as if the anger and emotional pain are bleeding out of the cut.

Even though the scars heal on the outside, the wounds go so much deeper. Those are the scars that don't heal, and they never fade. I lean over, grab the large Band-Aid from the bag, and stick it over the cut. I wipe my leg and begin cleaning up.

"Zara!" Knox yells.

I pull my shorts down on my hips to hide what I've just done, but it doesn't hide as much as I would like.

"Zara!"

I zip up the bag, unlock the door, and rush out. "I'm here."

Reaper and Viper's heads are poking out of their bedroom doors. Viper smirks when he sees me. Knox's face instantly relaxes, and his shoulders visibly slump as he exhales deeply. He strides toward me.

"I needed the bathroom," I say quietly to not wake anyone up, though I think Knox just did.

Viper mumbles, "Knox, ya psycho. Go back to bed." He closes his bedroom door.

Reaper studies Knox and waits. Knox lifts his chin, then Reaper shuts his bedroom door.

Knox's eyes search mine. Then, like a light switch turned

on, he stares at my thigh. His muscles tense and a deep frown curves his lips. He pulls me into his arms, where I sag into him.

Knox tenderly kisses the top of my head and lingers before he pulls away. He lowers himself into a crouch and inspects the bandage. He clears his throat. "Let me know if you need another one," he says before he stands. There's no missing the sadness in his voice.

My belly growls loudly in the silence.

His eyes widen as he peers down at my stomach and then back to my face. "Come downstairs. I'll grab you something to eat."

"I'm not hungry." His gaze sharpens. I put up my hand in a stopping motion. "Please, I can't eat. I'll throw it up."

He rubs a hand through his thick black hair, concern apparent in his eyes.

So I negotiate, yet again. "One piece of toast."

"Thank you."

After breakfast, my phone pings with a new message.

Boss

Thinking of you today.

I stare blankly at the message. I never know how to act and how to reply.

Thank you.

Ava walks into the living room, yawning.

I cringe. "I hope we didn't wake you."

She jumps, then grabs her chest when she looks at us. "Sorry, I'm still half asleep . . . I usually get up around this time to get a start on breakfast." Her body stiffens and her lips curve into a deep frown as recognition dawns. She rushes to me, bends, and puts her arms around me in a big hug. "I'm so sorry, lovely."

I wrap my arms around her. "Thank you."

"If you need anything, I'm here."

She moves to the kitchen, and it isn't long until I hear sizzling and smell bacon.

The other women appear next, looking as tired as I feel. They make their way to Ava. I go to stand to help, but Knox grabs my hand and shakes his head. "Don't worry about it . . . not today."

The men file down the stairs, one after another. I gather the smell of food has gotten them swiftly into their seats. As the women bring the dishes out and lay them on the table, I'm amused by the looks on the men's faces. A mix of appreciation and hunger.

"Fuck yeah!" I peer up to see Axle and Elena walking in, hand in hand. "I'm starved. My woman kept me up all night." His lips twist into a naughty smile, while Elena's face goes red.

"Axle, I beg of you, no details," Ava pleads.

He jerks his head. "Yes, queen."

Reaper strides toward us and leans down to kiss Ava on the cheek. When he pulls back, his eyes dart around to everyone before they pause on Knox, then land on me. He gives me a sad smile. He doesn't have to say anything. The sympathy in his eyes is unmistakable.

Reaper leaves, going toward the back of the house. I listen to the chitchat around the table until I hear "Conan!" from outside.

I stand in curiosity. Ava and Elena rush out the back door, so I follow them to see Reaper chasing Conan around the backyard. Reaper is fast, but Conan's bolting at full speed with what I presume is Reaper's shirt in his mouth.

I laugh as Ava cackles and Elena is bent over in a fit of laughter. Knox is chuckling to himself. Axle and Viper are next, bursting from the back door. We watch as Reaper leaps off to the left, missing Conan by an inch.

"Go, Conan! Go, Conan!" Axle hollers next to me, waving his arm.

Reaper stops and throws his hands up. "I give up! That dog is a pest!"

When Reaper reaches us he's still breathless. Ava gently puts her hand on his back. "I'll get you another clean shirt."

His adoring gaze is a lovely sight. "That would be great. Thank you, beautiful." He kisses her cheek.

A bit of jealousy bubbles up inside of me. *I wish I had that with Knox.*

"That was fuckin' fantastic. Conan," Viper yells, "you never disappoint!"

Conan is still gripping the shirt in his mouth, and by the looks of it, he won't be giving it up anytime soon.

Axle elbows Reaper. "Maybe next time."

Reaper shakes his head at him. "I don't know what else to do. The dog hates me."

"He'll warm up to you soon," Ava coos as we all walk back inside.

"Ha! Highly doubtful," Axle replies.

Ava's eyes narrow at Axle. He shrugs. "What? It's true."

I smile at them. They remind me of the bickering and jokes from when I was young with Knox, Misty, and Kane.

AFTER MY SHOWER, I PUT ON LIGHT MAKEUP AND CONCEALER under my eyes to hide my restless night. I spend the day in the living room watching trashy TV that the women have put on. Anything for a distraction, but it's good chilling out, spending time with everyone.

"Who do you think the father is?" Candy asks.

"Her husband's best friend for sure," Twitch replies.

Mercedez is in his lap. She turns to him, nodding. "I think so too."

I watch the TV as another man walks onto the stage. The crowd gasps and cheers. The husband stands. He gestures at the man while looking at his wife. "Who the fuck is this guy?" The woman's hand flies to her mouth.

The presenter steps toward the new guy and leans over. "Why don't you tell him and the audience who you are?"

"I'm the guy she's been fucking for the last ten years."

The crowd cheers.

Rage's hands come up in disbelief.

The husband strides toward the man, his face full of anger, though two huge security guards dressed in black-collared shirts beat him to it and hold him back. "You asshole! I can't wait until I get my hands on you!"

I stand to get fresh air. Knox tugs at my wrist, so I peer down at him. "I'm going to go outside for a bit."

He holds eye contact and slowly nods.

I remember that there's a dog outside, so I move to Ava, who glances up at me.

"The dog's name is Conan, isn't it? Does he bite?" I ask.

"Yes, that's his name." Ava smiles. "No, he's fine with women."

"Why is that?" I ask softly, not wanting to cause too much of a distraction to the others watching the TV. "Is he aggressive toward men?"

"If he senses a threat, he will react. He's wary of men at the beginning, but after a while, he's fine."

"Thanks," I mutter.

I make my way through the house and step outside. Heat

from the sun meets my skin, instantly warming me. I look over at Conan, who has lifted his head and cocked his ears. When his eyes land on me, he wags his tail. As I walk toward him, he stands. I halt and allow him to come to me. He circles me, sniffing at my legs and feet. I put my hand out. He sniffs my hand, his nose cold against my skin. Then he licks me and nuzzles his head into me.

I pat him softly, but the more I pat him, the more he leans into me. I chuckle and step toward the table and chairs. "Come on. Over here, Conan." His tail wags faster, and he follows me. As I take a seat, he positions himself in front of me, leaning in seeking more affectionate touches.

The back door opens and Knox walks out, though I'm not surprised to see him. As he makes his way to me, Conan rolls over, so I bend and pat his belly up and down in long, slow strokes.

Knox sits next to me. "I've called Kane. He'll be here soon."

I sit up. When my focus shifts to Knox, Conan whines.

"How did Kane sound on the phone?"

Knox frowns and looks away. "Like himself, though I doubt he'll be able to fake tonight, which is probably why he didn't want the vigil to take place."

"I can't say I was too thrilled about the idea either, but if Mom needs it, I'll be there. Did Kane mention whether your mom was coming tonight?"

"She is, but she won't be staying long. Kane said she'll be leaving afterward."

I briefly shake my head, wishing she was staying longer. It will please Mom that Audrey is at least coming.

"What about your dad?"

"He wouldn't miss it."

There's another whine next to me. Conan lies on his belly, looking up at me with sad eyes, as if he has never had a pat in his life. Sympathy wells up inside of me, so I slide off the seat and sit cross-legged next to him on the ground and return to patting him.

"Spoiled dog."

I smile up at Knox. "He is a little needy."

Knox puffs. "A little?" he asks, with amusement in his tone.

Conan stands and leaves a long lick of slobber up my face. "Awe." He licks again, so I put my hands over my face and giggle, but the more he licks, the more I laugh.

"That's enough, Conan." Knox's voice is stern, so Conan stops and backs away.

Knox stands and bends down to offer me his hand. I place my hand in his and he helps me up. He kisses it above where the ring is that he gave me. "Let me hold you . . . support you . . . Let me be your person today. You can go back to hating me tomorrow."

I gasp, then pull out of his hold and stand on my toes, looping my arms around his neck. "I don't hate you," I whisper into his ear as his arms come around me, holding me firm against him.

He left an imprint on me when we were only kids. That has never lessened.

I faintly hear the back door close.

"Umm . . . Bomber."

I pull away from him.

We turn our attention to Twitch. He peers at the ground, then back at us. "Uh, sorry, but your brother's out the front, waiting."

Knox and I glance at each other. "I need to grab my bag and wash my face," I tell him. He nods. I wait until Twitch leaves to say, "You can be there today, and to be honest, I'd struggle without you." He was always my safe space.

Knox gives me a stiff nod, though I notice his shoulders

fall. He follows me inside and places his hand on my lower back, making me shiver. When I get to his room, I pick up my bag from the floor, go to the bathroom to wash my face, add a little more makeup, then make my way back to Knox, who hasn't moved from the bottom of the stairs.

"Are you ready?"

My heartbeat quickens. *No*, but I reply with, "Yes."

As we move through the house, Knox stops to talk to Reaper, but I keep walking out the front door.

Kane is leaning against the limousine. When our eyes meet, I see a flash of pain in his. Like Knox said, he puts on a front, but I can tell he feels the pain like I do.

We walk to each other. My vision blurs with tears as I step into his warm embrace. When we shared this day together, he and Knox made it bearable. Sometimes, sharing the pain with someone rather than internalizing it is comforting.

We step out of the hug and I brush my tears away.

"I'm glad you're back," Kane admits.

I clear my throat. "Me too."

He tilts his head toward the idling limousine. "Let's get going."

Kane opens the door and slides across the leather seat. The front door of the clubhouse opens and Knox walks out. With his eyes on us, he swiftly moves to the limousine. I shuffle over as he sits next to me and pulls the door shut.

Kane knocks on the glass panel between us and the driver, then the car moves forward. Apart from the gravel crunching under the tires, there's a heavy silence between us. My chest pounds with the relentless beating of my heart. I lift my hand to my necklace and drag the heart charm across the chain over and over again.

Knox places his hand on my leg. He squeezes it in support. I glance at Kane. He's frozen in place. His shoulders are hunched and he's peering out the window blankly.

Arriving at the amusement park makes my pulse spike. The car pulls up at the entrance, and I look up to see the familiar large clown face that covers the entryway. Knox opens the car door and gets out first. I follow and wait for Kane. When he doesn't come, I bend down to look inside. I give him a quivery smile because I understand his hesitation.

His lips are curved into a deep frown. When I look into his eyes, his fear distorts my vision. "I get it's hard, but it's only us today. We can focus on celebrating the life we had with her. Tonight is the time we can let out all our other emotions." He stays seated, so I add, "Please, Kane, *I* need *you* today."

It wouldn't be the same without him, and I'd like to think today would bring him a sense of closeness to her.

He reluctantly slides across the seat and gets out. Knox threads his fingers through mine, and I grab hold of Kane's hand with my other to pull them up the stairs and toward the entry. This is what Misty and I used to do: grab their hands and pull them inside.

But this time, it's just me.

After I get the VIP passes, we walk through the entrance and toward the rides. Everything looks the same, even though I haven't been back in a long time—the smell of the food, the sound of the carnival music, and kids laughing in the background.

I look back at Kane. "Are you okay?"

His shoulders and torso loosen. "You're right . . . I'll do my best to focus on the positives."

Kane looks around, then walks toward a cotton candy cart. He talks to the man, who is wearing a navy-blue uniform. The man passes him three cotton candies, one for each of us, and Kane strolls back and hands me and Knox a stick. I pull off a piece of the pink cloud and put it in my mouth. The super-sweet cotton candy hits my tongue, and it's heavenly. Misty and I would eat this all day until we felt sick.

Kane's eyebrow rises while he watches me eat. "Good?"

"So good," I mumble, and a small smirk tugs on his lips.

We walk around the park, bypassing all the children's rides, and before I know it, my legs have taken me to the ride I see in my dreams. I can't stop staring at the carousel as I watch the young children travel around on it, smiling and laughing.

I hear a chuckle beside me and look at Kane.

"Out of all the rides, she liked this ride the best. The little kids' ride." He grins, remembering the past, and my heart warms at his smile.

My body stiffens as I spot the back of a young woman riding on the carousel. She has long, straight, blond hair. When the ride turns and she faces us, my chin dips and my shoulders drop in disappointment. It's not Misty but a woman with her young child.

Knox puts his arm around me and rubs my arm in soothing motions. I look up at him and can't stop the tears from falling down my face. I slump into him, my head resting against his shoulder. Every time I see someone who resembles Misty, I experience a surge of hope in my chest. Until I find out the truth about what happened to her, I'll always search for her.

THIRTEEN

MEMORIES BRING HER BACK

Knox

I LET OUT A HUGE BREATH AS THE SAFETY HARNESS OF THE RIDE lifts above my head. As I slide out of the seat, when my feet land on the base of the ride, the rush fades. Zara and Kane are smiling, and I follow them off the ride and onto the ground. I stride up to them.

The thrill rides provide a short high, but being on my motorcycle, that's a real rush. Being on the rides brings me back to when we were kids, and even I can admit it's been worth it to see them both happy, even for a while, before the hell that tonight will bring.

It's late afternoon, and I want Zara to eat something decent before tonight, as she always struggled to eat when she's upset.

I tilt my head in the restaurant's direction. "Follow me." I know if I tell them about going, Zara might put the brakes on and refuse to eat.

It's only a short walk until we reach the restaurant that

overlooks the water. It's a tapas bar called the Decadent Flame, where we used to go when celebrating events and birthdays when we were kids. When we reach the entryway, I dare to glance at Zara. She stares at me with her lips pressed into a hard line, but she doesn't object, so I take that as a win.

We walk in and as we reach the hostess, the woman's eyes bulge when she looks at me. Her eyes travel from my face to my cut, and she licks her lips. "Knox, we weren't expecting you." She peers over my shoulder. When her gaze falls on Zara, her eyes widen even more.

"Zara," she says in an exasperated tone. She moves from behind the podium and steps to her, throwing her arms around Zara.

"I should have known you'd be back in Crown Village. After I finish here, I'll be going to the vigil."

"Thank you, Shelly," Zara replies. I realize we went to school with the woman.

"I'm sure some more news will come to light tonight," says Shelly.

Zara's face falls, though she answers her. "I hope so."

They pull apart, and Shelly points to a table. "I have a four-seater available. I'm glad you came now. It was very busy at lunchtime."

I'm not surprised. The place always used to be packed. As we follow her, I look around. It's been a long time since I've been here. It's been renovated. The atmosphere is intimate, with dark lighting and a mixture of plush easy chairs and tall wooden tables. The new furniture, maroon walls, and high, dangling light fixtures create an atmosphere that is both modern and luxurious.

When we sit, Shelly hands us the menus and smiles before walking back to the front of the restaurant. A waitress arrives at our table, and her eyes flick between the three of us. "Would you like a drink?"

"Crown Village whiskey with cola," Zara answers.

I look at Kane in time to see him flinch, as if her words brought him pain. Though, soon after, he gives her a heartfelt smile. "Me too."

"Make that three," I tell her.

The waitress nods. "I'll go get them for you now."

There's a comfortable silence between us. I follow Zara's eyes out the window. It's been a hot day. The sun is reflecting off the water, and the waves are lapping the shore in slow motion.

Kane picks up the menu. "I can't pronounce half the meals on this."

"Did you want anything in particular?" I ask Zara.

She scans the menu. "The fish tacos look good. So does the pork belly."

Calmness washes over me. She's hungry.

"We can get those. Kane, why don't you order a mix of dishes, and then we can all pick at them?"

Kane's lips pull up into a wicked smirk. "Absolutely."

The waitress comes back with our drinks and places them in front of us. "Are you ready to order yet?"

"We are," Kane replies.

She pulls her pad and pen out. "What would you like?"

"Come here, I'll point to them. I'm not even going to bother trying to pronounce them."

Zara smothers a laugh.

The waitress steps toward Kane, who's holding the menu and pointing to what he wants. "That one, two of that one." She nods as she scribbles them down.

Zara's eyes are on the ocean, her hand touching the glass. "I forgot how beautiful the view is from here." Instead of the view, my eyes latch onto the ring on her finger. A sliver of warmth lightens my chest that she's still wearing it after all this time.

Kane leans back in his chair and peers at Zara. "So what else have you been up to?"

"I've been really busy with work, and apart from that, I occasionally help at the local homeless shelter when I can."

Fuckkkk! We have gone on two very different paths, almost the opposite of one another.

Her eyes bounce between the two of us. "What else have you guys been up to?"

Kane looks at the ground, then rubs his chin. "Not helping at a homeless shelter, that's for sure."

"I wasn't expecting you to," she says, smirking. "How's the casino going?"

"It's always chaos. Each day, I never know what I'm going to walk in on or what drunk asshole I'm going to have to deal with."

Zara shifts, giving me her full attention. "What about you? What do you do for work?"

I don't even have to look at Kane to know he has a stupid, smug grin. When I glance at him, I see I'm right. He raises a brow, as if curious to know how I'm going to answer her.

"I don't have a day job. I'm sergeant at arms in the MC."

She squints at me. "But how do you earn a wage?"

I pause. "I can't divulge that information. It's club business."

Kane doesn't even know what we do, but he's not stupid. He knows we earn money by doing something illegal.

An awkward silence hangs heavy in the air. I can't tell her. She would have to be my ol' lady before I can give her details, and even though I've been saying to everyone that she is, she's really not. No civilian can be half in and half out. We can't afford for anyone to let slip that we grow and distribute weed.

"Are your cousins still living here?" Zara asks us.

Our cousins hung out with us during the holidays when

they came home from private school, but then we all grew up and did our own thing.

"Yeah," I answer Zara. "Alec, Lawson, and Harrison are still here. Sophie moved away a while ago."

"Are they coming tonight?" she asks.

"They are. I'm not sure about Sophie, though," Kane replies.

The waitress brings our drinks and sets them in front of us on the table. "Food won't be long."

Zara raises her glass. "To Misty." We pick up our glasses and clink them.

"To Misty," we say in unison.

Shortly after, our food arrives. There's a comfortable silence as we eat. I glance at Zara every so often to check that she's eating. When we finish the food, we chat among ourselves.

As we leave, I pull out my wallet and open it. Kane gives me a weird look. "We aren't paying."

Shelly smiles. "Yes, family is free."

Zara steps up next to me and gasps when she sees the photo section of my wallet. I watch her closely as she takes my wallet from me, bringing it closer to her face to get a better look.

"Can I take this out?"

I slowly nod, watching her expression. She slips her finger in, pinching the photos and sliding them out. There's two of them. Two of Zara, one recently and one before Misty left— before the pain tainted her.

Her brows pinch. "How long ago was this one?"

I look away, thinking. "Six months."

Her eyes widen. "You really came to see me." She frowns. "I wish you would have actually spoken to me." Her voice conveys her longing, underlined with sadness.

I clench my teeth as guilt churns my stomach. "You were better off."

"No, I wasn't." Her voice breaks.

My shoulders fall and my chest is heavy. *Did I make a mistake? Should I have gone to see her and spoken to her?*

As we walk out, my phone rings in my pocket. I pull it out to see Reaper's name. I answer it immediately. "Is everything all right?"

He lets out a deep chuckle. "Everything is fine. I was calling to tell you we just arrived."

I pull my phone away from my ear to see that it's five thirty.

"Who's that?" Kane asks.

"Reaper," I mouth to him.

"Oh . . . Tell him they should allow everyone to come in for free now for the vigil."

"Did you hear that?" I ask Reaper.

"Yes. See you soon," he replies.

"We'd better get going," Zara says, her anguish obvious. "Mom is probably already here."

Kane's shoulders fall. I wish I could take their pain away from them. I know I need to look into Misty's disappearance again, for everyone's sake. "You two go ahead. I need to make a phone call."

They pause. Zara nods. Kane searches my eyes, interested in who I'm calling.

"I'll tell you later," I say quietly. I wait until they leave, then I call Alec.

He's my cousin on my mom's side. He practically manages all his father's businesses in Crown Village, and if anyone can get the ins and outs, he can because nothing happens in this town without my uncle and Alec's say so.

"Hello, Alec speaking," he says in a professional, monotone voice.

"It's Knox."

"My apologies for today. I might be late to the vigil, but I'll get there when I can."

I'm grateful my family is coming. "I appreciate it. Can I ask a favor?"

"Anything."

"Can you investigate Misty's case for me? I'm going to try to get more answers tonight, but I want to go over everything again. Something has been missed. Someone knows more than they are letting on."

"Sure . . . It's been playing on my mind since Helen approached me about having the vigil. Ten years, I can't believe it. The vigil is all everyone's been talking about. Everyone's going, so be prepared for a crowd. All my family should be there soon to pay our respects—even Sophie traveled for it."

Having the family back together with Mom and Dad, just like old times . . . I wish it were under different circumstances.

After we hang up, I search for everyone. When I see men with cuts on huddled around the carousel, I walk toward them. They all turn to look at me when I arrive.

Reaper squeezes my shoulder. "The women and some men are getting the supplies from Zara's mom's car. What do you need from us?"

I tip my head. "Thanks, pres. When they get back, I'll ask Zara's mom, Helen."

Viper steps toward me, gives me a bear hug, and slaps my back.

"Did you want me to check the crowds?" Demon asks. "See if there's anything suspicious or watch out for anything out of the ordinary?"

"Yeah, actually." I've got my hands full with Zara. At least I have the men to fall back on. They will step up if I need them to, especially Demon. He nods and leaves us as he strolls. A woman pulls her child closer and gives Demon a wary stare when he walks around the back of them.

Rage, Cash, and Axle walk to the tables with big brown boxes in tow, women trailing.

"What's the boxes for?" Viper asks me.

"I have no idea."

The men put the boxes down and make their way to us, while the women open them. Zara pulls out a pamphlet. She studies the front of it. Her fingers trail over the image. When she opens it, she wipes away tears. I step toward her, but both women dash to her side. Elena puts her arms around her waist, pulling Zara to her, as they all peer down at the pamphlet.

I've appreciated the women helping around the club-house, but I've never truly valued their kindness and support until now. They're there for Zara, when they don't even know her.

"The women have got her back."

I glance up at Reaper and let out a heavy breath. I clear my voice. "It means a lot."

"That's not all. We purchased hot dogs, rolls, and some sauces, and we'll grill some hot dogs for the people attending."

"You didn't need to."

"My woman insisted. You know what she's like."

I hear a sob and peer up to see Zara holding Helen. Their arms are wrapped around each another. I look up at the sky, wondering why bad things happen to good people. Zara hugs her dad next, and I make my way to them. I peer over my shoulder to see the men following me.

When we reach them, Helen leaps into my arms. "Oh, Knox," she says, and I wrap her tight. When she pulls back, she wipes her nose with a tissue, which she then puts back in her pocket. When she lifts her eyes, they widen at the men surrounding us.

Reaper steps forward. "We're here for you. Whatever your family needs."

Helen steps to Reaper and puts her arm around him. She looks so small next to him. He puts his arms around her. "Thank you," she says, then looks around at all the men. "I'm thankful for all of your help."

Viper puts his arm around her shoulder. "Bomber's family is our family." John introduces himself to each man, shaking their hands, then Ava and Elena fuss over Helen. I've never been prouder than I am today to wear the club's vest and patches.

Kane makes his way to us and stands beside me. "Who did you call?" he asks with a raised brow.

I turn my back on everyone else and lower my voice. "Alec. I'm not settling for what we already know about Misty's disappearance anymore. I'm looking into it myself, and Alec is going to help. The police might have missed something."

Pain etches his face. "Are you sure you want to bring all of that up again? We would have found out when it happened with all the resources we had."

"Actually, I do. The Pratt family needs answers, and I'm going to do whatever it takes to find out what happened." I gesture toward the crowd. "Look at all the people here already. Her disappearance rocked our community just as much back then as it does now."

Kane lets out a deep sigh. "Okay. I'm with you, every step of the way."

My eyes land on our mom, who strides toward the Pratts. Helen lets out a squeal, and they embrace each other.

"Well, she showed up," Kane deadpans.

"Mmm . . ." I grumble.

It's not good enough. I lost all respect for her a long time ago.

Twitch steps to us. "Hey, I heard Helen mention needing to set up the sound equipment and projector." He peers over at Zara's parents. "I can do that for them."

"I'll show you where it is and help you," Kane replies.

They stride toward the hall.

Mom's eyes land on me, and I groan when she walks my way. Her arms come out for a hug, but I take a deliberate step back. She frowns and her arms fall.

"It's good to finally see you."

"Well, whose fault's that?" I reply bluntly.

My once-confident Mom breaks eye contact and looks away briefly before glancing back up at me. She used to be covered in diamonds. Her hair was always tied back in a bun, and she wore the most expensive brands. She's none of that now. Instead, she has black jeans and a long black shirt on. Her face isn't full of makeup, and her hair is back in a ponytail.

I peer around her, seeing no guards with her. "Where's all your security?"

Something flashes across her face but quickly disappears. "There was no need for them to be here."

There was never a need for them. She's just paranoid. "Is the one-million-dollar reward still applicable?"

She slowly bobs her head. "It is."

"Good."

Another motivation for people to help.

"It's been ten years. I doubt any new information will be found."

My eyes narrow at the stranger in front of me. "You don't know that."

"Where's Kane?"

I glance to the hall, where I see Kane and Twitch with their hands full. I tilt my head in their direction. "Helping with the sound equipment."

"I'm going to make myself useful."

I grab her arm as she goes to leave. "What was the private investigator's name?"

She stills momentarily. Then her mouth falls open. "Why?"

"I want to ask him some questions."

She blinks rapidly. "Knox, it was a long time ago. You can't expect me to remember."

"I need for you to look into it for me."

"Why?"

The frustration in her voice makes me grind my teeth. What a stupid question!

"Just do it. It's the least you can do."

Her eyes narrow and she pulls her arm out of my grip. "Don't talk to me like that. I'm still your mother."

I shake my head. "Nah . . . my mom died a long time ago."

Harsh but true.

She gasps and covers her mouth, but I walk away. She left when we needed her. I don't recognize who she's become.

I look around at everyone working together. Kane's setting up the sound equipment. Twitch and Helen talk while looking at a laptop on the table. Rage and Axle are off to the side, handing out the pamphlets. Elena and Ava are getting the candles out.

I see John talking to my dad. We make eye contact, and I give him a small wave. My dad smiles and waves back.

"Bomber." I shift to face Viper. His eyes are bulging. "Who's that?" He points into the crowd, but there's a lot more people here now and I can't decipher who he's talking about. "Who?"

"The blond bombshell."

The side of my mouth curves when my eyes land on her. "That's my cousin Sophie."

She's off to the side, talking with my other cousins, Harrison and Lawson.

"Do you mind if I . . .?" He gives me a suggestive brow raise.

I scratch my head. "I wouldn't."

His jaw drops. "Why?"

"She will eat you alive."

He laughs. "I fucking hope so."

I chuckle, knowing how feisty Sophie is. "Not even you are a match for her."

He groans and runs a hand down his face. "Is she into women?" He smiles. "I think I can turn her."

"She's not into women. Well, not that I know of."

Viper smiles smugly. "I think I can handle her."

"Don't whine to me when it all goes to shit." When we were younger, she left a long trail of broken hearts everywhere she went.

He whacks my back. "Sweet! How long is she going to be in Crown Village for? You'll have to introduce us."

I shake my head. *Idiot!* He can't help himself thinking he's God's gift to women. It will be entertaining to see him try and fail miserably. "I'm not too sure how long."

I search the crowd for Zara. She's talking to Iris. I go to them, and when I reach Zara, I press a kiss to her temple. She looks up at me and smiles, then I glance at Iris. "Hey."

She grabs my cut. "What's this?" She clicks her tongue.

"What do you think it is?" I ask her.

"Trouble!"

We laugh together.

"Can I see you before you go?" I ask Iris. "I want to ask you a few questions."

Zara tugs on my hand. "I'm meeting up with her tomorrow if you want to come."

My eyes flick between the two of them. "I will. If you don't mind."

"Zara!"

We turn to Helen. "It's time . . ."

Zara's breath hitches and she bows her head.

I lace our fingers together, bring her hand to my mouth, and plant a kiss above her ring. Her eyes soften, but I let her hand go so she can be with her parents. The crowd goes quiet when "Memories" by Maroon 5 plays.

The projector is showing a photo of Misty that was taken prior to her disappearance. Helen passes out roses to Zara and John, and they walk over and put them by the projector. Elena and Ava go around with their lit candle, lighting others.

When the song finishes, Twitch hands Helen the microphone. She looks out at the group. "I'd like to thank everyone for coming out tonight."

As she says a prayer, I peer at the sky. There's only a small beam of light left from the sun as it descends, and apart from her voice, it's quiet besides the rides in the background. As I glance at everyone, I see Reaper off to the side, speaking to Parker, the police officer. There's a line of my MC brothers around the back of the crowd, paying their respects.

"Please protect my baby girl, Misty," Helen says, with tears streaming down her face. "We miss her every second of every day." She chokes on her words, and even I'm having trouble keeping the tears at bay. I stride toward them, linking my hand with Zara's once more. "Did you want me to talk?"

I had no idea what I was going to say, but I hated seeing Helen breaking down.

Zara shakes her head. "No, I will . . ." She looks at me with glassy eyes. "Can you come up with me?"

I squeeze her hand in support.

"Okay . . ." she says through a breath.

We step to Zara's parents, and Zara gently takes the microphone from Helen's hands. Helen sags into John.

"Heavenly Father," Zara begins, glancing up at the sky, "protect Misty, my sister and best friend. Please watch over her and guard her from evil. Give her the courage to return to us, to reunite us . . . because she has left a hole in my family" —she looks at her parents—"in her friends"—she looks at Kane, then looks back at the crowd—"and in the community." She takes another deep breath. "Help us find out what happened to her. Grant us peace. Amen."

I wrap my arm around her waist. While holding her, I reach for the microphone. She passes it to me as she buries her face in my chest and cries, and every tear shreds me. I turn to her parents before talking into the mic. "Do you want to talk again or . . .?"

John replies, "Zara said everything that needed to be said."

I bring the microphone to my mouth. "For those who don't know me, my name is Knox. I'm a close friend of the family. Again, we would like to thank everyone who has come to pay their respects." I search the crowd and wave Parker over. "If anyone remembers anything leading up to or on the date of Misty's disappearance, no matter how small, please speak to our local police." I wait for Parker to join me. "This is Officer Parker, and he will record the information."

I'm aware no one will come forward if I ask them to talk to our MC, and at least I can get feedback from Parker.

"Don't forget there's still a million-dollar reward for information that leads to finding Misty. Now, please join us for hot dogs, provided by War Brothers Motorcycle Club."

Once we get back to the clubhouse, I wait for Zara's lead to see what she wants to do. She pulls on my hand to go up the stairs, so I follow her down the hallway and to my room. Once the door closes, she lets go of my hand and throws her arms around my neck. The pain in her eyes levels me.

"Please, Knox, just make me forget," she whispers with a breathy plea.

I pull her closer, my arms around her back. I lower my head and take her mouth with a promise of what lies ahead. I'd give her the temporary relief she needs. As our mouths open and our tongues meet, I tilt my head, tasting her with slow, deep licks.

A sexy moan leaves her. The sound of her pleasure reverberates through me, firing into a blaze that had lain dormant since I was with her last. I bring my lips to her neck, placing delicate kisses along it, the way she used to like it. She shivers, then her head falls back, giving me better access.

I've waited so long for her that my hands are shaking. There's a desire to shred her dress, but I resist and step away from her to kick my shoes off. Her breathing is quick and harsh. She watches me as I take my jeans off, then rip my shirt over my head and toss it on the floor. My boxers are next. Her gaze flits to my cock, and she doesn't hide the hunger in her eyes.

Her dress and underwear are next. The faded light from the moon and stars seeps through the blinds casting shadows over her ivory skin. Every curve, every inch of her, is just as flawless as I remember. We're breathing heavily, her chest rising and falling, and my own.

I move to her and cup her face, my eyes piercing hers. "I love you," I breathe.

Her mouth opens into an O, so I capture her lips again, not wanting to hear the rejection. I'm helpless against the way she makes me feel.

As my tongue delves into hers, I run my fingers feathery light down her throat, down her side, allowing my hands to tighten their grasp on her hips. The kiss fuels the passion inside of me. She presses into me like she needs me as much as I do her. We walk together toward the bed, never breaking apart. When the back of her legs meets the bed, she falls, and I fall with her, bracing myself with my arms to ensure I don't crush her petite frame.

Nestling my hips between her thighs, she spreads her legs wide. My lips return to hers and I ravage her mouth again. Our tongues stroke each other in feverish desperation. I kiss her, letting her feel how much I've missed her. Her perfume wafts over me, making me hungrier.

Blood rushes through my veins. The anticipation of sinking into her has me struggling to hold back the need to claim her. "Are you on the pill?"

I want to take her bareback. No, I fucking *need* it.

"Yes," she answers against my lips.

I inch back. "I want nothing between us. Are you okay with that?"

I need her consent, even though my cock is twitching to be inside her. I'm desperate to feel her around me . . . raw.

Her entire face is soft. She looks at me with hooded eyes. She nods, her tongue snaking out, wetting her lips. "Yes."

Need, sharp and painful, surges.

Grabbing my throbbing cock, I drag it through her heat. She draws a breath through those full lips. Her hand drifts between us, curling around my dick, giving it a firm squeeze, a warning.

I lift her leg up over my hip. I enter her swiftly, then slowly push myself all the way into her. Zara gasps. She is tight and hot, and she clamps down on me. *Fuck!* I stay that way, letting her adjust. Barely holding on to my control, I drive in and out. Thrusting deep and slow, I work her. Her slick wetness coats me. Seeing her nipples erect, I have to have them. I lean down, my mouth capturing the tight bud. My tongue swirls greedily, teasing, tasting.

She exhales. "Knox."

I love the way she says my name.

When I pull back, I knead her breast possessively. She looks sexy and wild. Her hair is fanned out around her head and perspiration licks her skin. As I pick up the pace, she matches my rhythm. The air pushes from my lungs in heavy spurts.

She arches her back. Her nails dig into my shoulders. I groan at the mix of pleasure and pain. She's close. I can feel little tremors along my cock. I've wanted to come inside Zara a million times over and then take her again and again. It would never be enough.

I pull out, then slam home. Zara mewls my name. Pulsing and soaking wet, she comes, and I follow her over the edge. I let the tip of my nose run up her clammy neck, and I place one more lingering kiss there, savoring her, never wanting this moment to end.

BEST
FR_ENDS

FOURTEEN
SECRETS AND LIES KILL RELATIONSHIPS

Zara

Waking up, I feel the warmth of Knox's body. The weight and heat of his muscular arm around me. The throb between my thighs is a reminder of last night. *He said he loves me.* My chest tightens at the thought. More than anything, I would love to let my walls down, but I can't. I still hold a wariness with him, terrified that he could shatter my world again. I won't survive it a second time.

I gently take his wrist and pull his arm off my body, then shuffle across the bed. When I reach the end, my eyes dart between his sweatshirt and my dress as I wonder what to put on to walk to the bathroom. When my feet meet the floor, I bend down and scoop up his sweatshirt. I pull it over my head, loving its warmth and the scent of his cologne.

I step to my suitcase and fumble through my clothes until I find my jeans and a casual shirt, underwear, a bra, and my toiletry bag.

"What are you doing?" he asks, making me jolt.

I turn and look at him. His eyes are skimming over me, the smallest smile on his lips. He nods, as if happy with my selection of clothing. The blanket is dangerously low on his hips. I jerk my head away to stop myself from checking him out. *Today is a new day. Everything is to go back to how it was.*

Looking back, I ensure my eyes meet his and not his body. "Thank you for yesterday." I didn't want to be ungrateful.

He stiffens, and he grimaces like my words hurt him. "Don't go back to treating me like a stranger." He sits up and turns his legs over the edge of the bed. He runs his hand through his hair. "Stay with me . . ." His voice is thick with pain. He stands with his arms out. "Stay with me . . ."

I know I'm not dying, but my heart's bleeding out. I turn my back to him and grasp the door handle. "I can't . . . I'm sorry."

After stepping out of the room, I gently close the door behind me. I briskly walk to the bathroom, tears running down my face.

Once I've showered, I feel more awake, but my body feels cold. My breathing quickens with every step to Knox's bedroom. When I open the door, he's sitting on the edge of the bed, his head in his hands. It makes me frown, and the guilt hits me.

I did this.

I want to reach out and touch him, comfort him, though I tightly grip my clothes to keep my hands restrained.

Knox thought I was doing better without him . . . but maybe he was just saying that to be kind . . . Maybe it was the other way around. He didn't want to get involved with me again. He didn't want to have to tiptoe around me and treat me like glass or be the one to lean on.

Being a burden is a heavy weight to carry. The guilt swells, assaulting me, so I sit beside him. He lifts his face from his hands.

His sad eyes pierce mine. "I never said this, but I'm sorry," I tell him. "I was in a lot of pain with Misty when she disappeared, and even though I was broken, I never asked you how you were coping . . . how you were feeling. So thank you for being selfless, and even though we broke up, I want you to know I did and still appreciate every time you've been there for me."

His eyes soften. Even though I wanted to keep my distance, my hand moves of its own accord around his waist to hug him, as if I were granting us this moment of surrender.

His arms envelop me, pulling me into him, as he tenderly kisses my head before he says, "You bleed, I bleed . . . remember?"

"I remember," I whisper, blinking back tears. I could never forget.

During breakfast, I make an effort to thank everyone again for their support at the vigil. Afterward, we put on our helmets and head for his motorcycle. He swings his leg over it and hops on. With his hand out, he helps me get on behind him.

"Hold on tight."

Excitement shoots through me. My arms tighten around him and we pull away. I can't stop smiling as we leave, slow at first and then racing off down the road, with the roar of the motorcycle between my legs and the howl of the wind biting my skin, making my hair flutter from underneath the helmet. There's a freeing feeling to being on the back of a motorcycle.

I shift my head to the side as I look at the view once we get closer to the main street of Crown Village. There are mountains in the distance, and trees and dense shrubs cover the land. I forgot how gorgeous the scenery is here. A mix of heritage and modern businesses greet us next. Most I'm familiar with, but there're new ones as well.

We ride closer to the shore and pull into the beach parking lot.

Happiness slides away and nervousness takes its place. My heart thumps as I get off the motorcycle, and my hands shake as I struggle to get the helmet off. Knox's hands gently fold over mine and he unclasps the helmet for me, freeing the straps, making me exhale in relief.

"Thank you," I say, handing him the helmet.

He doesn't answer, but the devotion in his eyes says it all. There's an ache at the back of my throat, and I'm finding it difficult to swallow. I shift, looking away and out along the tree line, where there are picnic tables. When I squint, I see Iris sitting at the second table closest to us, so I walk to her. My stomach drops further with every step, unsure about what this conversation will bring about Misty's disappearance.

When we reach her, she stands and smiles, and I walk into her outstretched arms. When I pull back, I notice the wrinkles around her eyes she's gained over the years. I sit as she gives Knox a brief hug. She sits across from me and fans her face as her eyes gloss with fresh tears.

I try to swallow again, but it's difficult.

"Helen did a spectacular job of the vigil. It was a beautiful ceremony," says Iris.

"It was. I wish Misty could have seen how many people were there and how many miss her." My voice is strangled. I rub the bottom of my throat. "It sounded like you wanted to talk to me about something."

"Yes," she replies, but she briefly peers out at the beach. "What did you get told about me leaving?"

I find that an odd question.

"You returned to be with your family." My eyebrows furrow. "Why, was there something else?"

Tears fall down her face. "Please forgive me when I tell you this."

I freeze. Everything quietens, and I focus on Iris. Every one of my senses heightens. I don't answer her . . . I can't. Heavy silence descends on us until she speaks again.

"Early on, when it was me, Audrey, and Helen in the kitchen, we were talking about where Misty could have gone, and we were throwing out suggestions on what could have happened. I told them I thought Misty was pregnant."

My world spins and I gasp for air. Knox shuffles over, his arms coming around me, holding me. "I . . . How?" I pause. "She was still a virgin. She would have told me . . ."

The sympathy in her eyes tells me otherwise. I shift and look into Knox's eyes. His sad gaze makes me shake my head at him. "She would have told me. We didn't keep secrets from each other."

He flinches, making me think I was wrong. An unsettling feeling takes hold of me. I pull out of Knox's embrace and shuffle away from him. "You knew?" I whisper with hurt in my voice. "You never told me."

His frown deepens. He puts his hand on mine, but I pull mine away.

"I told Misty and Kane to tell you they were, but they didn't get around to and then she went missing. Kane told me they were using protection, so I thought nothing of it." His eyes narrow at Iris. "You don't know she was pregnant, and you have no proof, so why bring it up?"

There's a bite in his tone, but they *both* were hiding secrets from me.

Iris lets out a long sigh. "She was vomiting every day. She had cravings. I knew she was having sex because I caught them. It all aligned, and it made sense to me. You say he wore protection, but nothing is one hundred percent effective."

Her words saturate my mind, though they feel like barbed wire twisting, making incisions into my heart.

"There was no reason for her to leave. She would have known everyone would have supported her."

She raises a hand. "Let me finish. Helen's eyes looked the way yours do. Denial that Misty would be having sex. Audrey was quiet for the first time in her life. I thought it was strange, but the next day, she approached me with her bodyguard at my home."

Iris's eyes dart between us and she visibly swallows. She takes a torturous moment, as if trying to keep herself together to continue. "Audrey had papers in her hand and asked if she could come in, so I let them. We went into the dining room, where we sat down, and she told me that my employment was terminated immediately. Your family needed time and space to be together as a family during the difficult time."

I tilt my head. "My parents told you to leave?" I needed her. *They wouldn't . . . would they?*

"I don't know if you're aware, but it was Audrey who helped me get the position. She has cleaners as well, so she had her lawyer draw up a similar contract to theirs for the Pratts that stated my terms and conditions. In that was a nondisclosure clause that Audrey reminded me about. She said to keep my opinions about Misty to myself and that they were not to be discussed with anyone or they would sue me. She was cold and clinical. I had never seen her act that way before, and it scared me. I told her I wouldn't tell anyone. I wanted to stay, but she was firm on letting me go."

"Did she explain why?" I'm quick to ask.

"She mentioned she didn't want Kane brought into the case and she didn't want her family's name tarnished because I had made up a rumor that wasn't true. She offered me a bonus for being a good and loyal employee but only on the condition I sign an updated nondisclosure agreement. I realized maybe she also thought Misty was pregnant and that she was paying me off so I wouldn't say anything, but another part of me had known Audrey for so long. I had trouble reconciling that it was a possibility."

I suck in a sharp breath that fills my lungs. *No . . . no . . . no . . .* I dare a peek at Knox. His face is pale, his eyes wide, his expression pained.

So many questions bubble up inside of me. "You took what she said as fact and didn't even see us or come say goodbye?"

"The conditions were clear. I wasn't allowed to contact any member of your family or hers. I needed the bonus payment. It was life changing. I could not pass up the opportunity to pay off my house, so I asked no more questions. I signed the documents. After months and years of reflecting, I had my suspicions she knew more than she was letting on. It was too coincidental that a day after I suggested Misty was pregnant by her son, she was at my house with an offer of a bonus in return for my silence."

"Who else did you say it to? Did Kane know?"

"No one, and I never spoke to him about it. If he knew, he didn't hear it from me."

"Why didn't you call the police?" I'm dumbfounded Iris had her suspicions but did nothing.

She shakes her head and gives Knox a pointed look. "His family is powerful, and I was scared. Her bodyguard was intimidating enough while in my house, and if I had gone to the police with only my suspicions, they would have laughed at me. Audrey's family has and always will have a direct influence on the police. I didn't know what Audrey was capable of, and I wasn't going to find out."

Her words are cutting me. It's all too much. My head pounds. I need to get away from her . . . from him . . . from everyone.

"Was there anything else you wanted to tell me?"

She reaches out to touch me.

"Don't."

I don't want her comfort. I understand, but it doesn't lessen the blow. She could have been honest a long time ago.

Tears fall down Iris's face. "No, there's not. If you need anything, even someone to talk to, please call me. My phone number is still the same."

I abruptly stand to leave. "Why tell me now?"

"Please don't bring up that I said anything, but after the vigil, I couldn't keep it to myself any longer."

"I won't. I'm leaving." I turn my back on her and walk away.

All these secrets and lies are like poison eating away at my relationships. I walk to the motorcycle in a daze. *Did I even know Misty?*

Knox grabs my wrist.

"Don't touch me!"

He flinches and his brows draw together as his hand falls to his side. "I had no idea about my mom . . . about any of it."

My eyes tighten, though I want to believe him. "How do I know that? All of you kept secrets from me! Was I delusional?" I throw my hands up. "I thought I was happy and everyone cared about me as much as I did them, but now I'm not so sure."

"I do—"

"No. I don't believe that to be true. Even Misty was keeping secrets from me. Hell, she probably knew she was pregnant too."

I pull my phone out, press on Mom's number, and bring it to my ear.

"Hi, is everything okay?"

"Are you free?" My voice comes out in a hurry.

"Sure . . . Where are you?"

I stare at Knox while I answer. "Can you pick me up from Crown Beach and take me home to get my car? I'll be waiting in the parking lot."

"Are you okay?"

I try not to cry. "Can you come now?"

"Okay, I'm leaving. I'll see you soon."

After I hang up, I tell Knox, "I'm fine. You can go."

He doesn't move. His body is rigid. "I'll wait until Helen gets here."

"No, I need space." I point to his motorcycle. "Just go."

He shoves his helmet on, swings his leg over the motorcycle, revs the engine, and peels out of the parking lot.

FIFTEEN

DANGEROUS TRUTHS

Knox

I PULL THE THROTTLE BACK TO ACCELERATE. MY HEART RACES.

Pain . . . Fear . . . Dread . . . One punch after another to my gut.

I'm going to be sick. Minutes later, I pull up outside the casino, throw my keys at the valet, and bolt to the garden. As I bend with my hands on my knees, vomit rises and I retch until there's nothing left. I've never been sick over my emotions, but Zara makes me feel everything.

I'm going to lose her again . . . What has Audrey done? When I stand, I take a couple of deep breaths, though my throat burns.

I walk to the glass entrance doors. They open wide, allowing me to stride inside. Two women with casino uniforms on are standing behind the stone counter.

"Hi, Knox," one says in an overly cheerful voice. I don't have time for pleasantries. I yank my phone out of my pocket and press Kane's number. When he answers, I say, "I'm at the casino. Where are you?"

"I'm in my office."

I hang up, walk to the elevator, and quickly and repeatedly press the button to call it to the ground floor.

When the doors open, a man walks out as I walk in. I swivel and press the button for the third floor, then swipe my access tag. No one but my family and managers are allowed on that level. As the elevator rises, I tap my leg. When the doors open, I step outside, march down the corridor, and yank my brother's door open. It bangs as it hits the wall.

Kane stands at his desk. "What the fuck, Knox!"

"Did you know?"

His brows furrow. "Know what?"

My chest heaves, but then a thought comes to mind. *What if he doesn't know, or what if Misty wasn't pregnant?* I choose my words carefully. "Audrey paid off Iris after Misty left. Did you know about it?"

Kane tilts his head, his eyes hardening at my accusation. "How would I know that?" He plonks down in his chair and leans back. "You're pissed off. Why? Why does it matter?"

"It matters because Iris told Helen and Audrey"—*she's not my mom anymore*—"that she thought Misty was pregnant." I focus on Kane. He gasps and stills. I watch for any tell that he knew, but he shakes his head.

"She wasn't pregnant."

"Well, Audrey turned up with her bodyguard the next day at Iris's house. Audrey said her employment with the Pratts was terminated and she was to abide by the terms and conditions of her employment, which included an NDA." The longer I speak, the paler Kane gets. "Then she offered Iris a bonus if she signed another NDA to not talk about the case to anyone and because she didn't want you,"—I point to him—"being pulled into the case."

"Don't point your finger at me, *brother*! I always wore protection. I'm telling you she wasn't pregnant."

"So there wasn't one time that you even started having sex, then put the condom on afterward? You know condoms aren't one hundred percent effective."

Uncertainty clouds his face. He shoves himself up out of his chair, which tumbles backward, hitting the wall. "It was a long time ago. I don't remember."

"You need to think real fucking hard. If there was even the slightest of chances Misty was pregnant, it changes everything. If Audrey paid Iris off, then she knew. She knew, Kane . . . all this time."

Dad walks in. "What the hell is going on?"

I pull my gaze from Kane and turn to Dad, who is standing in the doorway. "Shut the door and come in," I tell him.

Dad pauses first, his eyes darting between Kane and me. He opens his mouth, but he says nothing and gently closes the door before turning to us. In my peripheral vision, I see Kane pacing by his desk.

"Did you know?" I ask Dad.

"Uh . . . know what?"

"Misty *could have been* pregnant."

He chuckles. "What are you talking about? She wasn't pregnant. We would have known about it."

"By the sounds of it, Audrey knew, and when Iris made a comment about her thoughts that Misty was pregnant, Audrey terminated Iris's employment and paid her for keeping silent."

Dad blinks repeatedly and looks at Kane. "Is this true?"

Kane stops pacing, turns, and leans on his desk with his hands, bowing his head. "I don't know . . ." he whispers.

Dad's hands come to his face, his mouth agape. A heavy tension fills the air.

Kane raises his head. "We were having sex. I knew she was sick, but I thought she had caught some bug," he says with undeniable sadness.

It all clicks together like a puzzle. "That's why Audrey moved!" My voice booms. "She and Misty moved to our holiday home. Audrey isolated herself, remember? It's why she has never invited us over and why she kept her distance. She didn't want anyone to know."

"But why?" Dad asks. "It's been ten years. If Misty was pregnant, there's no reason to stay hidden. Something doesn't make sense. Let's go now!" He stomps his foot. "We need to demand answers."

I put my hands out. "No! If Audrey and Misty hid this long, we don't know what Audrey's capable of. She could leave the state—hell, the country—if she wanted to. As you said, something isn't right. We need a plan, and we need to execute it carefully. I don't want to spook her, and we still don't know for sure if that's what has happened."

There's a thump. Kane has collapsed. Dad and I rush to him. It's as if he fell to hold himself steady.

Tears fall down Kane's face. I haven't seen him cry since Misty left. His anguish pains me.

Dad is by his side, his hand on his shoulder. "We're here for you. We will find out the truth."

"What if she was pregnant?" Kane sobs.

It's a soul-crushing sound. I know I'll never forget it. I turn to leave.

"Where are you going?" Dad yells out.

I clench my jaw. "To find Kane some fucking answers."

With every step, the anger washes over the pain, digging in its claws, and I embrace it. My breaths come short and quick. I crack my knuckles on the way out. If what I think is true, when I find out who has helped Audrey and Misty keep their secret, they are going to pay. I'm the sergeant at arms for a reason.

AFTER GETTING ON MY MOTORCYCLE, I RIDE TO THE CROWN Resort. My cousin Alec is the CFO and also lives in the penthouse, so I'm sure he's in the building somewhere. First I go to his office and stride past the receptionist and other staff, ignoring his personal assistant, who's telling me I can't go into his office. I open the door to see my cousin in a meeting with another man.

Alec's eyes narrow, but then he studies my face. He stands and looks at the man on the other side of his desk. "Sorry, James, we will have to reschedule."

The man stands and nods, gives me a wary glance, and goes around me to leave.

"I'm sorry!" the PA says from behind me.

"It's okay, Mandy. Close the door on your way out."

When she does, I ask. "Did you look into Misty's case?"

He straightens his tie. "Take a seat."

My heart crashes against my ribs. "I can't. Tell me what you found out."

He sits, opens a drawer in his desk, then pulls out a manila folder. He puts it on his desk and opens it. "I'll warn you now. You're not going to like it." His lips tighten. "There was hardly anything on Misty's file for her disappearance. Which I thought was strange." He scatters the documents across his desk. "There were interviews with family, friends, schoolteachers, her biological family, and basic information about her case. I expected more since the case was linked to our family. Her case was on TV and Audrey had a reward out, but there was not one eyewitness after she left the Pratts'."

I rub my face. "It makes no sense, and I'm desperate for answers or even a lead."

He gives me a sharp nod. "I agree. So I did some digging. The lead investigator on the case has resigned and now lives with his wife in a house in the suburbs in Crown Village. However, it's only his wife's name on the deed of the house."

"How did they afford that?"

"I had someone look into both of their financials for me. I only got them back this morning." He looks back at the papers and grabs the sheet on top. He passes it to me, but I don't take it.

My hands are clenched by my side. I'm too wound up. "Just tell me."

His shoulders fall. "Years after Misty's disappearance, the investigator's wife purchased a house outright, so it's only her name on the deed, and then the investigator resigned."

"You think the cop got paid off . . . so they purchased the house with the money but put it in the wife's name to avoid what would look like a payoff?" I pause. "It was Audrey." It had to be.

Alec tilts his head. His hand goes to his chin. "Why do you think it was her?"

"I don't want to go into it right now. Can I have the lead investigator's address?"

He passes me the piece of paper. "It's on that. And Knox?"

"Mmm . . ."

"If Audrey had anything to do with it, tread carefully. Regardless, she's still my dad's sister. And trust me, you don't want any blowback from him or our family." He and Audrey own most of the large establishments in Crown Village. They are wealthy, and with money comes power.

I shrug, then walk out.

I don't give a shit.

WHEN I GET BACK TO THE MC, I PARK BETWEEN VIPER AND Demon. It's a sunny day, so the men are outside cleaning their motorcycles. I pull my helmet off. Viper has stopped cleaning and is staring at me with a raised brow, wipe in hand. He opens his mouth as if to say something, then slams it shut and stands.

Demon stands too. They know something is wrong. I step to Reaper. He wipes over the handlebars, but when I get close, he peers over at me and slowly stands up.

"I need a church meeting," I tell him.

He takes a second, then nods. "Church."

Everyone stops what they're doing. I feel their curious stares as I move inside. Ava is wiping down the entryway table as I walk in. She gives me a small smile and looks behind me, then frowns. "Where's Zara?"

I shake my head at her, make my way to the computer room, and peek inside. "Twitch, church."

He swivels in his chair to face me. "Yeah, coming." He stands and follows me out.

Once we've gathered the rest of the MC, we stand around the table, with Reaper at the top, me and Viper at his sides, and the rest of the club around it.

Everyone sits.

"Bomber, you have the floor," says Reaper.

"First, I'd like to say thank you to every one of my brothers for being there for me during this difficult time." Reaper leans over and puts his hand on my shoulder. "I called a meeting because I found out more information in relation to Zara's sister's missing persons case, but before I go further, before bringing all of you into this. I wanted to call a vote. This isn't club business," I say as I look around the table, "so leave now if you don't want to be involved. I won't have any hard feelings toward any of you."

I make eye contact with every single member, giving them an out, but no one leaves.

"I live for this shit!" Demon says from beside me.

I knew he would be with me. Keen to get his hands dirty.

"Zara and I contacted an ex-employee who worked at the Pratts' when Misty disappeared. Once she suggested Misty was pregnant with my brother's child, she was paid off by Audrey, my mom, and was made to sign an NDA to not speak about the case to anyone."

A mix of grunts and gasps sound around the table.

"I went to visit my father and brother, Kane, who did not know about it. Then I went to see my cousin Alec. He had done his own digging for me and said there wasn't enough done about the case. The lead investigator purchased a home outright in Crown Village. Alec and I drew the same conclusions—that he was most likely paid off. I know it was Audrey, but I wouldn't mind paying the investigator a visit."

"Yes!" Demon says beside me, rubbing his hands together.

"Why would your mother do that?" Viper asks.

"She cared about her reputation, and if she found out Misty was pregnant, I know she wouldn't have approved. I don't know what happened, but it can't be a coincidence that soon after Misty's disappearance Audrey left to go live at our holiday house in the mountains and never returned. We thought it was odd, but we put it down to her being a coward and wanting to get away from everyone's grief."

"A police officer, even in retirement, couldn't afford a home in Crown Village," Cash chimes in.

"You know," Twitch says, "I looked into the statistics of

missing persons cases, and when it comes to teenagers, acquaintance kidnapping is comparatively high for women compared to your stereotypical kidnapping where the person doesn't know the perpetrator."

Axle squints at Twitch. "Only you would look at statistics in your spare time . . . ya nerd."

I didn't even consider kidnapping as a possibility. I look at Reaper. "Did you hear from Officer Parker?"

"Yeah. There was nothing worth mentioning," Reaper answers.

"I need to work with my brother and Zara on this, so I'll have to bring them into the fold, update them on what's going on. Raise your hand if you are okay with this."

Everyone raises their hands.

"What are you going to do about your mom?" Axle asks. "Do you think Misty's there, or what's going through your mind?"

"I don't know about that part. I want to face Audrey, but she's a flight risk. I might scope out the property tonight. If I confront her, it needs to be by surprise, and I want it planned out to ensure there're no mistakes. I can't let her get away without an explanation. And on that"—I glance at Twitch—"can you get me house plans and any information on the security of her house and anything else you can think of?"

"Where's your girl?" Viper asks.

My throat gets clogged, so I shake my head.

"I'll manage all of this. You go get your woman!" Viper replies.

"Thanks," I say, appreciation clear in my tone.

"When am I visiting the pig?" asks Demon. I know he's referring to the lead investigator of the police.

I pull the piece of paper from my pocket and pass it to him. "You can watch his house. Check back and make sure he's there, but you can't go in . . . not without me."

His wicked smile dims. "Shame, how long are you going to be?"

My lip lifts at his eagerness. "Hopefully not long." I'm going to get *my woman* first.

BEST
FR-ENDS

SIXTEEN

THE CUNNING PUPPET MASTER

Zara

I COULDN'T GO INSIDE MY OLD HOME, AND I DIDN'T WANT MY parents to see my unrest, so I drove to the lake instead. I'm in the parking lot, watching the boats and people walk along the trail on the shore. So many emotions strangle me. I'm scarcely aware of the tears falling.

I slam my hands on the steering wheel.

Why was everyone hiding the truth from me? Misty . . . Knox . . . Iris . . . Audrey . . . *Did my parents draw the same conclusion that Misty was pregnant? Did Kane know? Has Misty been hiding from me and my family all this time? How could she do this to me?* I slam my hands again as a tormented scream bursts past my lips.

My phone rings. I stare blankly at the lake. My phone pings with what's most likely a voicemail message but then rings again. I shuffle through my bag, moving my wallet out of the way to see my phone lit up with Knox's name. My thumb hovers over the cancel button but presses the answer button instead. I remain silent, waiting for him to talk.

"I'm sorry." His voice is thick with emotion.

"Tell me . . . what else do you know that I don't? No more hidden truths."

"Nothing . . . but I've been to see Kane, Dad, and Alec to get some answers."

I sit up straight in my seat and listen carefully, hanging on to every single word Knox says.

"Alec said there wasn't enough done on Misty's case, but the lead investigator somehow paid for a house in Crown Village. My senses tell me it's why Audrey moved away and paid everyone off to not look into the case. Audrey put up a million-dollar reward, and even though she has the money to back it up, she knew no one would come forward because she paid Iris off and paid off the investigator to turn a blind eye to any important information that comes their way."

I pause, allowing the news to sink in. "What about Misty? Do you think she was pregnant and they both moved away? Why would they do that? Misty loved Kane. If she was pregnant, I don't see her moving away from him. I'm hurt that Misty thought she couldn't confide in me and was hiding stuff from me, but I still have trouble grappling with the idea she left us to go with Audrey of all people. I can't say Misty was her biggest fan." Misty's carefree nature did not go down well with Audrey.

"I agree with you. Can I pick you up? I'm working on getting answers. Demon and I are visiting the lead investigator tonight, so please come back to the clubhouse."

I hesitate. "Okay," I answer softly, eager for more information but still unsure on where I stand with Knox and how I feel. "No more surprises, okay?"

"No more surprises. But there are some things I want to

talk to you about. Where are you? I'll come pick you up now."

"I need my car, so I'll drive to the clubhouse."

There's a gush of air through the phone. "When are you going to get here?"

My chest warms at his need for me. "I'll see you soon, Knox."

I drive to the clubhouse, faster than I should. I pull up off to the side of the house so that I'm not blocking any cars or motorcycles in. Knox waits for me, leaning against the pillar on the porch.

As I open the door and stand, he rushes over, stands next to the car, and pushes my door closed for me. He wraps his arms around me and pulls me to his chest. My body tenses. He pulls back and cups my chin in his hand, forcing eye contact. His stare is intense.

"The only thing I knew about was Misty and Kane sleeping together. Nothing else. I promise."

I stop resisting and embrace him, tightening our hold as he kisses the top of my head.

"I'm sorry, so sorry, precious."

I blink rapidly as I force those emotions down and pull back. "What are your plans next?"

"Me and Demon are going to see the investigator tonight. Twitch is looking into the house plans because I want to visit Audrey, to catch her off guard, but that won't be tonight. I wouldn't mind capturing her security guard. He would know what's going on or what happened."

I've noticed him calling his mom by her first name. "That security guard has been by her side for as long as I remember."

"Yeah," he answers, glancing away. "Pretty sure they were having an affair and that's why my parents split."

I rub his back. "I'm so sorry."

"I heard Dad slip up in conversation once, but there was no need to bring it up again. Dad's happier without her."

"What's with the security guard, anyway?" I ask.

"Audrey's always felt she needed one, whether it's because of our wealth or because she somehow thought she was popular enough to need one.

"Come inside." Knox tilts his head toward the clubhouse. I follow him in a daze, though catch sight of Ava and Elena by the front door, as if they're waiting for me.

Ava's lips curve up into a big smile, her eyes brightening. "Are you okay?" mouths Elena.

Their compassion and empathy makes me smile back. "I'll catch up with you two later."

Knox and I move briskly up the stairs and to his room, where he shuts the door behind us. We sit on his bed as I think back, linking Audrey as the main denominator. As if the jigsaw puzzle was slowly coming together, revealing the story. My brain zaps. "Well, I guess that's why Audrey sorted out a psychiatric center in the city for me."

His frown deepens. "She paid your fees as well," he answers.

I gape. Anger surges through my veins. He places his hand over mine. "She encouraged me to join the military and . . ." He looks away from me, before turning back with eyes full of emotion. "I believe she influenced your parents to make us break up, with the intention of sending you to the facility to keep you away from Crown Village, and from uncovering the truth."

I shift backward. "My parents asked you?" It was as soft as a whisper. "Why didn't you tell me?"

"Everyone, including myself, thought you needed it, and I told you . . . I will always put you first."

His selfless act saved and destroyed me. "If only you had told me, I would have still gone and we could have stayed together."

His eyes search mine. He doesn't look convinced. "Tell me the truth. Would you have left to go if we were still together?"

I lean back, away from him. "I guess we'll never know. You took that choice away from me." There's an undercurrent of frustration in my voice, but I deserved to have a say in our relationship. I shouldn't have had it forced on me without my knowledge.

A small, bitter laugh escapes him. "I've done *everything* in my power to protect you."

My mind scatters. "Protect me? You left me . . ."

"To save you!" He raises his voice.

I shake my head.

"You were physically harming yourself. Zara, what did you expect of me?" He stands and throws his arms up as his gaze goes directly to my thigh. "I was nineteen, trying to be there for you but then struggling to be there for Kane. He was always drunk, and then you cut yourself." He pats his chest. "I was drowning . . . failing everyone around me. I thought I wasn't enough for you . . . I couldn't be the person you needed."

My. Heart. Cracks.

I hurl myself at him, looping my arms around his stiff body. "You were exactly what I needed! You always have been." His body softens and he puts his arms around my waist.

I'm in a constant state of pushing him away and pulling him closer again. I inch back. Our gazes lock, my voice tight as I speak. "I thought you broke up with me because you didn't want me."

"It was the hardest thing I've ever done. I nearly couldn't go through with it." He chuckles, but there's no humor in it.

"I knew you were in pain, and I'm sorry for hurting you, but you needed help. You're still cutting . . ."

There was no judgment, just sadness.

I pause, thinking about how to answer him, then clear my throat as my heart constricts. I rub my thumb over the scars on my thigh. "They are my battle scars of depression . . . from the deep sadness of losing Misty. Every cut is a year of guilt and shame, like a million what-if scenarios ran through my brain. 'What if I had stayed home with her? Would she still have left? Should I have made her go to the doctor's earlier?' I could see all the shrinks in the world and understand why I do it and that it wasn't my fault, but it's not enough. It doesn't take the pain away."

He hugs me tighter and his fingers touch my arm in a soothing motion. "I love you. Never doubt that."

A rush of warmth fills my chest. I'll never get sick of him telling me that. He loves me, even knowing how damaged and broken I am.

"I love you too," I reply, my voice thick with emotion.

He nuzzles my neck and takes a deep breath, giving me goose bumps. "I'm obsessed with your perfume," he says in a raspy voice.

A smile tugs at the corner of my lips. "I'm going to go see Ava and Elena."

His shoulders fall.

I frown. "What's wrong?"

"I want to spend time with you without all this other bullshit."

I stand. "I hope that time will be soon." I bend, put my hand in his, and tug him to his feet.

We walk through the hallway and down the stairs. Knox turns and walks toward the computer room as I search for Elena and Ava. They're by the pool table.

Axle leans close to Elena. "You have to bend more," he

says. "Keep the cue near your waist . . . your waist," he reiterates. "Elena! Where's your waist?" His patience is gone.

Cash is suppressing a laugh.

Ava sees me and rushes over. Elena places the cue on the pool table. "Don't you speak to me like that. I'm not playing anymore," she mutters with her head held high. She sees me, her eyes widen, and she walks over.

"Oh, c'mon, baaaabe," Axle says. "Don't be like that!"

She peers over at him with narrowed eyes. "No! Don't *you* be like that!"

When Axle sees me, he tilts his head in greeting. "Good to have you back."

"Thank you!" I reply, noting the relief I feel being back here.

"Hey, Zara," Cash says in a friendly tone.

I give him a small smile.

Rage saunters in with a case of beer on his shoulder and walks to the bar.

"Did you get my wine?" Elena calls out to him.

He gets up from putting the beer on the floor and glances our way. He raises his head; his hair falls back out of his eyes. "Yes, I did. I got you two," he says, his eyes darting between Elena and Ava. "Four bottles between you. Is that enough?"

Axle chuckles and answers for them. "Hell yeah! I'm getting lucky."

"Yes, it is, thank you, Rage." Elena's eyes flit back to me. "Axle's a handful!"

I crack a smile and peek at Axle. "I can see that."

"I got your whiskey too." Rage says.

I look up to see his eyes on me. I swallow hard and feel a hand on my arm.

"I'm sorry. I didn't know what else you drank, so I made sure there was enough whiskey here," says Ava.

"Thank you for thinking of me."

"I know what it's like to feel out of place here," Elena says, but Ava finishes.

"We wanted to make sure you felt welcome. No matter what happens, we would love to exchange numbers with you. We don't have any real friends, and it's hard to find genuine people these days."

My hand goes to my heart. "I'm flattered. I would love to catch up again."

I've missed having friendships with other women. I have people I work with, but I've never found a bond like the one I had with Misty. I know I never will, but I need to stop comparing my friendship with her to my friendships with others. These women are here now and seem like lovely people to build one with.

"Did you want to go outside?" Elena asks. "Somewhere a bit more private."

We follow her out past the kitchen and out the back door. Conan raises his head and wags his tail when he sees us. When we step down closer to him, he stands with his long tongue hanging out. We all pat him as we walk to the table and chairs, and he trots beside us. When we sit, he sits in front of Ava.

"He's like a big gentle teddy bear," I say to them.

Ava laughs and rubs behind his ears. "Yes, he is," she replies.

Conan groans with enjoyment and leans further back into her.

"How are you?" Elena asks.

My lips press into a line. "I'm struggling, if I'm being honest."

"You don't have to tell us anything, but know that if you need to talk to someone, we're here for you."

I pull my phone from my pocket and pass it to Elena. "Can you both put your numbers in my phone?"

Elena grasps the phone and types away on it, then passes it to Ava.

"There's so much going on, but it looks like my sister and Knox's mom, Audrey, left together. Audrey now lives in their holiday home in the mountains, so we think that is where Misty is. But then again . . . I don't know how much you know about Knox's family, but they are very wealthy. Audrey could have taken Misty wherever she wanted."

"I knew the clubhouse is on Bomber's land," Ava points out.

"If I was that rich, I'd be living it up somewhere on a beach, drinking wine." Elena shakes her head. "How do you feel about the news that they left together?"

My throat tightens. "It hasn't been confirmed yet, but it hurts. I thought me and Misty were close . . . but the more information that's uncovered, the more I don't think I knew her at all. The Misty I knew would never leave her family and Kane."

"That's Bomber's brother, isn't it?"

I give Elena a sharp nod.

"All I know is the police officer managing Misty's case did a poor job and purchased a home in Crown Village, which his wife paid for in full. So we're thinking he got paid off by Audrey."

"Isn't Crown Village expensive to buy in?" Elena asks.

"Yes, it sure is. Your everyday worker wouldn't be able to afford it."

Elena's nose crinkles. "So . . . someone gave him hush money. Is that what you're saying?"

I nod sharply. "We think so."

She lets out a heavy sigh. "I'm sorry, it's a lot to take in. I can't even imagine how you must be feeling. How are you and Bomber?"

I blink a few times. "I don't think I'll ever get used to everyone calling him Bomber."

Elena bops her head. "I felt the same with Jake. Axle, like the axle on a motor vehicle, as a name sounds ridiculous."

Ava clears her throat. "No, Reaper wins hands down!"

Me and Elena laugh. "I don't know. Bomber's not that great." I look away, thinking about the rest of their names. "Demon and Rage aren't that crash-hot either." We laugh again. "Sorry, I lost track of what we were saying."

"You and Bomber," Elena answers.

"We are . . . I'm not sure. Everything's a mess. We have talked about how we feel and about the past. He told me things I never knew about. I appreciate his honesty."

"But?" Elena questions.

"What happened in the past, that pain of him leaving me . . . That wound is still fresh, even now. He told me why he left, which has made a difference—I know he still cares."

"He doesn't just care," Ava points out, "he loves you."

"I agree," Elena says.

"It's in the way he looks at you. I told Reaper a while ago that I was worried about Bomber . . . sad even that he didn't want to find a relationship with anyone."

Relief washes over me, but then Elena snorts. "True. He only paid for sex."

My eyes bulge. "What? Paid?"

Both women flinch.

"I'm sorry," says Elena. "I shouldn't have said anything."

Ava inches closer to me. "Reaper said he only paid for sex because it was a transaction, nothing more."

I sigh, knowing that I should have known he slept with others. "Don't worry about it," I tell them. "I guess I should be grateful he doesn't have a wife and kids by now."

Knox is busy talking to the men. But in between, no matter where I am, it isn't too long until he finds me to make sure I'm okay.

After helping the women with dinner, I go upstairs with Knox for privacy. When I jump into bed and under the comforter, I stay seated. "Did you find out anything?"

He gets in beside me and lies on his side. "The investigator is still home. Demon's been keeping watch. I'll meet him there soon to find out what he knows."

Relief and anxiety clash inside of me. I want to find answers, but at what cost? "And the cop's going to freely give up that information?" Suspicion coats my voice.

"Oh, he will," he replies confidently.

I nibble on my bottom lip. "What will happen to him?"

"Don't ask questions you don't want the answer to."

Oh, what the hell! "No more secrets. What are you going to do . . . intimidate him?"

Knox grunts. "More than that."

"Hurt him?" I ask, cringing.

His eyes scan my face as he watches my reaction carefully. "We will. Does that bother you?"

My shoulders fall, my hands clench the comforter.

He sits up and puts his hand over mine. "Think of it this way. If he was a decent human being, he would have done his job and we wouldn't be where we are now. I think we would have had a much clearer picture of what was going on. You, and my brother"—he shakes his head—"could have had answers a long time ago."

"I know," I whisper. My stomach sinks. "Will you and Demon be okay? Won't the retired cop have a gun?"

"There's nothing to worry about."

He's self-assured, but I'm not. The thought of him getting hurt makes me feel physically ill.

"Is there anything else you haven't told me?" I ask him.

"Twitch has got the house plans and is working on the security system as we speak. I want to pay Audrey a visit. See if Misty is there."

"I'm coming!"

"Afterward." His tone is sharp.

I frown. "What do you mean by that?"

"Once we have the security down and any security guards taken care of. *Then* you can come inside."

"No!"

His face and body turn to stone. "Well, that's what's happening."

I shake my head. "It's not, actually. It's important to me that I'm there. I want to see Audrey's and Misty's faces when we find them."

His face softens and he releases a deep breath.

My lip curves in a victorious smirk. "I'll take that as a 'Yes, I can.'" I'm relieved there's no more pushback. "What about Kane?"

"I'll call him tonight when I get back. I don't want him getting involved yet. His emotions make him unpredictable."

I nod, then glance away, knowing Kane will be as torn up as me.

"I heard about the escorts."

His eyes widen and he frowns. "Since I've known you were in Crown Village, I haven't seen them."

Them . . . I flinch.

"Hey . . ." he says, cupping my chin. "It's always only been you."

I nod in acknowledgment. "Since we're being honest, can you tell me what you do as a job in the MC?"

"If I tell you, you're not allowed to talk to anyone about it."

My pulse skyrockets. "I promise."

"We earn money by running and managing an illegal fighting ring, here at our warehouse, and we grow and distribute pot."

My mouth twists. "Is distributing marijuana dangerous?"

"It's nothing compared to running guns or hard drugs and having to deal with the mafia or a drug lord."

"I don't like it," I blurt out.

"You don't have to like it, but you have to accept it because it's what we do to earn money, and it won't be changing anytime soon." His voice is firm.

I look around the room, considering his words. Who am I to come back into his world and tell him what he shouldn't be doing? He's a different person now. He accepts me the way I am. I should accept him as well.

"I'm sorry for judging you and the MC." The butterfly painting on the wall captures my gaze. I can't help but ask, "Why is there a butterfly painting here? It seems out of place." As I fixate on the intricate details of the artwork, a sense of awe washes over me. "It's truly extraordinary."

Looking closely, the butterfly isn't perfect. Its wings are damaged, and it's missing scales.

"I had a young local artist paint it for me."

My eyes bulge. It looks like it's from someone who has been painting all their life. "How young?"

His hand comes to his chin. "When he did this, he was in high school. His name is Jackson. He tattoos now. If you see murals around Crown Village, they're from him."

"He's gifted. But wait, why did you ask him to paint a butterfly?"

A thoughtful look crosses his face. "You don't know?"

My brows furrow. "Should I?"

"It was my reminder of you."

My lip trembles as I look at the broken wing again.

He sits up and leans in closer. I can feel his warm breath on my neck. "Beautiful . . ." He places a soft kiss on the bend of my neck, making me shiver. "Survivor . . ." Another lingering kiss. "Mine." His voice is thick with lust.

I turn to him. His expression is dark.

"Yours," I whisper. The connection we share is soul deep, and no matter how much time has passed, it hasn't changed a thing.

He cradles my face and his mouth is on mine in an instant, making my eyes lazily drift closed. His lips are soft and greedy. When I part mine, his tongue slides in, taking . . . taking and taking. Heat gathers between my legs. He leans over me. His weight pushes me down on the bed, though our lips never break away.

He rises and I whimper at the loss of contact, but then his hand goes to my shorts. He unbuttons and I lift my hips. He yanks them down, and then my thong. I'm breathless. My heart's pounding in out-of-control beats.

His hands skim my hips before he grasps my shirt and shoves it and my bra up to reveal my breasts. Desire swims through my veins, but when his mouth wraps around my nipple and sucks, the desire morphs into need, creating a deep ache below. He lifts my shirt over my head and unclasps my bra. His eyes rake over me, the heat of his gaze making me feel sexy.

When he sits up, I watch him yanking his shirt off over his head. My eyes greedily roam over every muscle and every scar. He unbuttons his jeans next. The sound of his zipper lowering fills the room alongside my beating heart and heavy breaths. He kicks his jeans off. His eyes are wild and hold no control.

I open my legs wide, welcoming him. He crawls up,

peppering kisses up body. He places two tender kisses over the scars on my thigh, then over my stomach. I embrace the heat and weight of his body pressing into mine as he moves, placing soft kisses between my breasts and up my throat. He slips his hand between us to reach my folds. A deep husky sound escapes his throat when he feels how ready I am for him.

He eagerly spreads my legs wider. The tip of his cock pushes in, forcing a harsh breath from my lips. I feel myself stretching for him, then he thrusts all the way in. He seeks my mouth and kisses me again. His tongue swirls with mine, a mixture of tenderness and passion.

He pulls out almost entirely, then drives inside of me with a guttural groan. I grip his shoulders before he thrusts again. His pace quickens.

"Say my name. Scream it for me."

The sound of slapping skin ricochets off the bedroom walls.

"Yes," I hiss through gritted teeth.

A sheen of sweat covers his skin as he mercilessly drives into me.

"Knox, harder," I beg.

My fingers dig into his shoulders as his thrusts become harder and more and more frantic. As he inches back, my eyelids flutter closed at the building pressure within me.

"Zara, open your eyes," he growls breathlessly. "Keep them open. Look at me."

I follow his command. His dark eyes sear into mine. I'm so close, so very close. Everything is buzzing and I'm gasping for air. Punishing stroke after punishing stroke, he slams into me. I hold him tighter as we approach our orgasms.

"Let go, precious," he utters against my lips.

Overwhelming heat rises through me. We cry out in unison as we come together and the warmth of him releases into me. My world turns to white. My legs quake, and I unravel as the blissful wave of pleasure washes over me.

We stay this way, catching our breath. I wind my fingers through his thick hair and gently stroke the back of his neck. It's just us in our bubble of happiness before the cruel reality of our situation filters through.

BEST
FRIENDS

SEVENTEEN

BLEEDING OUT

Zara

Knox's phone rings on the side table. He leans over and looks at the bright screen. I dare a peek and see it's Demon.

Knox answers, listens for a second, and then says, "I'm on my way."

Alarm shoots through me. He gets up and puts on black jeans and pulls on a black shirt and a plain black hoodie.

"Do you have to go?" Worry is clear in my voice.

He bends over the bed and pecks my lips. I'm tempted to grab him, pull him down to me, and not let go.

"Yes, I do. I need to find out as much as I can."

"Can't Demon just go?"

"He won't know what questions to ask, and he can get"—he cringes—"uh . . . carried away."

I swallow hard.

He points to his cut, which is on the chest of drawers. "I'm sergeant at arms. This is who I am now. My job even within the MC is to protect and defend the club, and that can get bloody, depending on the threat."

I break eye contact, hating what he does.

"We'll be back soon," he replies, his voice softening.

When he leaves, he closes the door. I lie in bed and wait for the sound of his motorcycle, but instead I hear a car.

I toss and turn as the hours drift by but can't get comfortable. I pull my phone from behind my pillow and press the home button to see that it's 12:00 a.m. It feels so much later.

I shuffle to the edge of the bed, then step to my suitcase. I pull on underwear, shorts, and a shirt. When I poke my head out the door, there's a light coming from downstairs, but no one else is around.

I quietly pad down the hallway. Deep chuckles come from downstairs. I pause, not sure whether to join them or go in the opposite direction toward the front door. I decide to walk to the men.

Cash, Axle, and Viper are drinking beers at the bar. Cash smiles and shakes his head. He shifts when he sees me and dips his beer in greeting. Viper and Axle swivel in their chairs to look at me.

"Can't sleep?" Viper asks.

"No. Unfortunately," I reply as I make my way to them.

Cash stands, pointing to his chair, offering me his seat.

"Thank you." I step up and onto the stool.

Cash walks around the bar. "Would you like a drink?"

I raise my hand. "No, I'm fine, but thank you."

My eyes flick between the three of them. "Do you know how long Knox is going to be?"

Axle lets out a low whistle. "It could be minutes . . . it could take hours."

Viper leans forward so that he can see me fully. "Do you want me to call him?"

I shake my head. I don't want to distract Knox. "It means a lot that all of you are getting involved."

"Anything for Bomber," Viper answers.

Their close bond, fills my heart with warmth. "So . . . how did all of you meet?"

"Bomber, Reaper, and I are the founders of the War Brothers MC. We met in the military," Viper replies.

I nod. "I remember Knox mentioning that."

"Me and Cash here were in the army together. We heard about the MC through some other veterans, so we thought we'd come down to check it out," Axle says, then chuckles. "And we never left."

"Just like a bad smell," Viper mutters under his breath. "Hey, Zara, do you know Bomber's cousin Sophie?" Viper asks.

I suppress a smile at the softness in his voice. "Yes, though we don't talk much anymore."

"What's she like?"

Axle slaps Viper's shoulder. "Knox said you had no chance man, give it a break."

Viper's head falls back. "I can't," he groans. "She's by far the sexiest chick I have ever laid eyes on."

"She's really smart. Did well at school, though was also a party animal," I answer Viper.

"Did you even speak to her at the vigil?" Axle asks Viper with a raised brow.

"I was going to, but . . ."

Axle laughs out loud. "Fuckin' pussy!"

Viper's eyes sharpen. He mock shoves Axle. "If she stays in Crown Village longer, I'm going to get Knox to introduce us."

Axle rolls his eyes. "What happened to you? Mr. I'm-so-confident."

"She's a challenge, but I'm up for it," Viper answers him, with apparent determination in his eyes.

Hours roll by. I get more and more impatient. I've moved from the bar to the living room, where I'm mindlessly watching the ads that play on TV this late. I grab my phone and press the home screen. Still no messages or missed calls.

A car pulls up outside. My heart races. I'm on my feet, rushing to the front of the house. I throw open the door and bolt to the garage, from which Knox and Demon are emerging.

The metallic scent of blood is in the air. My eyes travel all over his body. "Are you hurt?"

Knox pulls away from me. "No . . . I need a shower." I stand still, watching as he leaves me to go inside. My stomach churns. Something's wrong. I stride after him and rush up the stairs. I peek inside his room, but he isn't in there. The sound of water running draws me to the bathroom.

I knock on the door. "Knox, is that you?"

"Yeah."

When I open the door, he's in the shower. His head is bowed to his chest. I can see every hardened ridge of his well-defined muscles. The droplets lick his skin and cascade over each corded muscle in his body. He hurt the retired cop to get information. I'm waiting for the guilt to come for the blood that's on my hands, but it doesn't.

Knox is quiet . . . detached. He knows I'm here but won't even look at me. I open my mouth to speak, but I don't know what to say. I'm desperate, but in his current state, I don't want to push him. I turn and go in search of Demon.

I close the door and pad down the hallway, to what I think

is Demon's room. I tap on his door; he doesn't answer. I hesitate. He shouldn't be asleep—he just got home.

I tap again, a little louder this time. "Come on in," he says in an amused tone.

My hand rests on the door handle, but my curiosity and need for answers override my hesitancy to walk in. I press down and exhale through my teeth as I walk in.

"Sorry to disturb you," I say as I open the door.

His bedside lamp is on, and he's lying on the bed with just sweatpants on. A swirl of tattoos covers every inch of his skin. He's staring at the ceiling, his arms under his head. The smell of blood is in the air.

I swallow down the bile threatening to rise, but then an uncomfortable thought flows through my mind. Even though Knox said he wasn't hurt, maybe Demon is.

"Are you hurt? Do you need me to get you anything?" It's the least I could do. He helped Knox.

Demon's face twists in pain. When he looks at me, his head tilts an inch to the side. But then he shakes his head and a wicked smile curves on his lips, though there's no mistaking the vulnerability in his eyes. That grin is his mask, and my heart aches at the thought.

He chuckles and says, "I'm alllll good. Though I can't say the same for the pig."

My body freezes. "What did you find out?"

"Ask Bomber."

"Zara." I hear my name being called from the hallway. I step toward Demon's door and open it wide to see Knox. His hair is still wet from the shower. His eyes narrow. "What are you doing in there?"

"Please tell me. What did you find out?"

He moves to me, grabs my hand, and starts tugging me outside, but I hold my ground. "Please!" The torment in my voice is unmistakable. Tidal waves of dread wash over me.

His eyes glow with anguish. "It was Audrey."

I look at him with bulging eyes. Pain fills my chest as though his words stabbed my heart.

"Misty and Audrey left together," he says, his face scrunching like every word is toxic.

"How do you know?" I ask.

"There was video footage of Misty at the pharmacy where she purchased a pregnancy test. Then there was video footage from the local retail store that's close to Audrey's house showing Misty's car parked outside, then again, with them leaving shortly afterward with Audrey's security guard. The officer never added the evidence to the file."

"So Misty's okay? She left me?" I ask as my world spins.

She actually left me . . . She near killed me. I was lifeless without her . . . without Knox. She was the hand holding the knife, cutting me open, and I was bleeding out.

BEST
FR-ENDS

EIGHTEEN

STRENGTH IN NUMBERS

Zara

I stare blankly at Knox, wondering how it got to this point. "How could they do this to me?" My voice stutters at the end.

With eyes full of sympathy, he steps toward me. He wraps his arms around me, though I feel cold . . . as if no warmth would ever penetrate. "I'm sorry," he whispers, then pulls me tighter. "I'm so sorry." His voice is raw, as if he did wrong and is apologizing for it.

I have an inkling to tell him it's not his fault, but my chest feels heavy and every inch of my body is cloaked with numbness.

He pulls back, his arms falling to his sides. "I have to call Kane."

I bring my eyes to his and nod.

"You want me to get everyone up for church or do you want to wait till the morning?" Demon asks from behind me.

I faintly hear voices, then see Axle, Viper, and Cash beside Knox. Their smiles fall, seriousness taking over.

"What do you need?" Viper asks.

Knox exhales deeply. "I've got to make a call."

Axle and Cash stay. Viper trails behind Knox. Axle peers at me and frowns.

Demons stands. "I'm going to wake Reaper."

"I'll help wake the rest and get everyone downstairs," Cash adds, and they leave.

"I'll be right back," Axle says.

It's just me, afraid to think . . . afraid to feel. I stand, gazing at the white wall in a dreamlike state.

Minutes pass and then Elena rushes to me. A deep frown mars her pretty face. "How about we go downstairs?" she whispers. She links our arms together. My legs move, but I feel disconnected from my body.

As we walk down the stairs, there's someone to my right, and I look to see Ava linking her arm with my other one. She gives me a sad smile, but the kindness of both women stirs something within me. We move past the men, who have congregated around the bar. I feel their eyes on me as we go toward the kitchen, where I sit on a stool.

"Where's Zara?"

I shift and peer over my shoulder to see Knox. His eyes roam over me, and he strides to me and kisses my forehead. "I've got to talk to the men. Kane's on his way."

Kane . . . he is going to be a wreck when he finds out. "What did you tell him?"

"Everything." He leans in, pressing another kiss on my lips before he leaves.

Conversations swirl around me. I'm aware of Ava making herself busy by going over and cleaning an already clean kitchen.

My fingers keep tapping on the stone countertop as I wait for Kane. The longer I wait, the more the anxiety pushes through the numbness.

A door bangs, and I whip around to see Kane. We lock eyes. His shoulders are hunched. I swivel the stool around, jump off it, and run to him, crashing my body into him. We hold each other tightly, as if holding our bleeding hearts together. That's all it takes for my vision to blur.

"I don't understand why they left." I inch back to look at him. Droplets of pain fall down his face.

"What if Misty had a baby?" His voice is strangled with despair. "I never got to hold the child, be a father. Instead . . . I'll be a stranger. They took my future from me. I would've been by Misty's side through her pregnancy. I would've supported her, done anything for her and the baby."

Pulling back further, I suck in a sharp breath. "We will find out what happened." That, I promise him.

Tears fall down my cheeks like rain. Knowing they've taken so much from all of us breaks my heart. We stay that way until the church door opens and the men walk out. Knox strides over. His eyes glisten as he sees his brother. I pull away, allowing them to hug.

"I want to keep you two updated with what's going on. Me, Viper, and Twitch are going to stake out Audrey's home to find out the extent of the surveillance and what security guards are there. Twitch got me the house plans showing the layout. I want to confront Audrey tomorrow night."

"When are you going to look at her security?" I ask Knox.

"Now."

"I need to go too. I can't stay here," Kane blurts.

"We are going to scope out the place. We are *not* going in yet," Knox exclaims.

"I realize that," Kane answers. "I still have to go with you."

Knox, Viper, Twitch, and Kane all get in a black van and leave. I helplessly watch as the van travels down the driveway and then the road. My shoulders drop as I make my way back inside. Elena and Ava stand when I walk in.

"Come watch some TV with us," Elena says.

Only Reaper and Axle are by the bar. It looks like the others have gone to bed.

I follow Elena into the living room. She sits and pats the seat next to her on the three-seater, so I sit in the middle.

Ava grabs the TV remote and passes it to Elena. "I'll be back."

Elena flicks through the channels, then turns her head to me. "What do you want to watch?"

I shrug, not having the mental capacity to think about it.

"I'll put a comedian on then," Elena says.

Ava comes back holding a blanket. She sits next to me and drags the blanket across us. This is what Misty and I used to do . . . and as if someone clicked their fingers, I'm transported to reality. She's the reason I'm feeling this way. *She's the reason for all my pain.*

Watching comedian after comedian make jokes, I'm struggling to focus on what they are saying, but then I'm distracted by the loud snoring that has started up next to me.

Elena turns and sits forward to stare at her sister. "Jesus Christ, it's like a freight train coming through the house."

My lip curves up as I smile. We peer at Ava, whose head is back on the couch. Her mouth is wide open as she draws in air, breathes out heavily, snorts, and gargles. It makes me giggle.

I can sense Elena's eyes on me, and when I peek at her, she has a warm smile.

"Reaper," Elena calls out. "Your ol' lady is snoring her head off. You might want to take her to bed."

Reaper and Axle make their way over. Reaper smiles at

Ava adoringly. He looks back at us. "She's been exhausted lately."

Axle bursts out laughing, his shoulders shaking. "She's got some pipes on her."

"She doesn't believe me that she snores," Reaper tells us.

"These women, I tell you what. They act all sweet and innocent at first . . . a couple of months later, it's all farts and burps, or, in your case"—he looks back at Ava—"snoring."

Elena gasps. "When have I ever farted in front of you?" she asks, sounding offended.

He raises a brow. "Are you serious, babe?" I'm not sure whether he's joking or not. "You literally *blow me away* in your sleep!"

I peek back at Elena. Her face is red. "You lie!" she spits.

Axle shakes his head, chuckling. "Nah, it's like you hold it in all day, then wait till we're in bed and then you just let it riiippppp. You're way too comfortable if you ask me. You think Ava sounds like a freight train, you sound like foghorn."

I feel immature, but I can't stop a laugh escaping.

"Well . . . I didn't ask you." She crosses her arms. "I call bullshit."

Axle puts his hand on Reaper's shoulder and looks up at him. "I think we are going to have to start videoing them."

Reaper chuckles and shakes his head. "No, Ava will be embarrassed. I'll take her to bed." He lifts the blanket from her and passes it to me. With an arm around her back and one under her legs, he lifts her and they leave.

I shuffle over, allowing Axle to sit between us so that he's next to Elena. He gives me a smile and sits.

"Do I really fart that much in my sleep?" Elena asks.

"I was exaggerating. You've done it twice."

She slaps his shoulder. "Why do you always have to embarrass me?"

He shrugs. "Because it's funny . . . and I love seeing you squirm."

Elena huffs. "Unbelievable."

Axle bats his eyelashes. "Yes, I am, baby," he purrs, putting his arm across her shoulders and pulling her to his side.

Another two hours roll by. Elena and Axle fall asleep on the couch. I'm wide awake, left wondering what the men are doing . . . and what they've seen.

Finally, a car pulls up. I'm on my feet and bolting to the front door.

Twitch is first inside, followed by Viper, who gives me a tight smile. Then Knox and Kane. I study their faces. Knox flinches when he lays eyes on me. Knox's and Kane's bodies radiate tension, making my stomach roll.

"I'm off to bed," Twitch says when he's halfway up the stairs. "Me too," Viper says, walking toward Axle and Elena. He wakes them up, gently shaking their shoulders, and they look at us.

"We will talk tomorrow," Knox says.

Axle yawns while nodding his head. He and Elena hold hands and walk up the stairs toward their room. I follow Knox and Kane to the living room. We all take a seat.

My heart races. I peer up at Knox. "What's going on?"

He releases a long deep breath. "There were no security guards out the front. Twitch could hack into her security, so he can disable it before we go tomorrow night."

"That was quick!"

"He's smart. He had a drone fly over and there was no movement within the property. Demon and Twitch are going to go there again tomorrow to see if there are any other security guards or anything we didn't catch tonight. I want tomorrow to go off with no issues."

I look at Kane, who looks disengaged. I don't even know if he's listening to us.

Knox puts his arm around my waist, bringing me close to his body. "It will all be over soon. You'll finally have your answers," he whispers in a reassuring tone.

BEST
FR-ENDS

NINETEEN
CONFESSIONS

Zara

Laying in bed my eyes wander over Knox's face. His whiskey-colored eyes reflect my own, with puffiness and dark circles underneath. We haven't slept; we lay together in silence.

"Should I call my parents?"

"No," he replies gruffly. "We can't talk to your parents until it's all sorted with the police, and it depends on what we find. Once there are no threats present, me, you, and Kane will approach Audrey and Misty, if she's there. If we need to inform the police, I'll call Parker, our contact at the police station. I can't have any of this falling back on the MC, so we can't tell anyone."

I jerk my head in a nod, feeling overwhelmed.

He leans in closer to me. "I need you to promise you won't say anything. The club is important to me."

"I promise." I wouldn't risk it. The MC is like family to

him, and he's loyal. The MC has become important to me too, especially the women.

THE DAY AND AFTERNOON DRAG ON. EVERY MINUTE IS TORTURE. I wish I could turn my mind off. I stretch out my sore arms, hoping for a reprieve. Every muscle aches from suppressing the dozens of emotions that keep crashing around inside of me.

At least it's now dark outside. "Are you coming with us tonight?" I ask Kane, making small talk, knowing the answer.

"You're coming?" he asks, surprised. "Knox is letting you go?"

I wrinkle my nose. "Yes, I'm coming, and Knox isn't my keeper."

"Have you asked him?"

My eyes narrow. "Kane," I warn. "I need to be there."

He looks away. "I know . . . I do too." His voice is heavy with heartache.

My eyes linger on the closed wooden doors to church. I wish I was in there with them, going through all the final details of tonight, but Knox said it's for patched members only.

"So you haven't said anything to your dad yet?"

Kane shakes his head. "Knox said I can't."

Silence descends. "Do you think he knew anything about Misty?"

"Our parents were fighting like hell for a while before the divorce, and that was before Misty went missing. They avoided each other at all costs. Dad's always been real with us. He would have told us."

He drifts off before speaking. "I'm questioning everything I ever knew about Misty. What was a lie? What was real?"

"What do you mean by that?" I ask him.

"I thought I knew her, but with every passing day . . . it's like I never truly did."

"Whatever the outcome, the relationship you had with her was real." I lean toward him. "You know it . . . you feel it here." I place my hand over his heart.

His Adam's apple bobs.

I drop my hands and sit up straighter in my seat. "There's no proof Misty's living there. Audrey could have helped her travel anywhere around the world. Regardless of the truth, there's still this part of me that can't believe Misty would leave us . . . that she would willingly cause us this much pain."

Kane's hands clench. "I'll forgive *no one* that was involved."

Doors open, and the men file out of church. Knox walks to us holding black vests. When he's close, he hands them to us. "They're bulletproof."

I open my mouth to speak, but he's quick to say, "Neither of you are coming unless you wear them. Go get changed into comfortable clothes and shoes you can run in."

It's finally happening . . . I feel like I'm going to vomit.

Both vans stop only minutes away from the property, out of sight of security cameras. Tension buzzes as we wait in the car. Everyone's dressed in black clothes. My stomach tightens at what's coming.

"Twitch, do it now," Knox tells him.

Twitch turns to us from the front passenger side. "It's done. The security has been disabled. I'll monitor it and keep you updated."

Knox nods, then talks into the walkie-talkie. "Demon, you there?"

"Sure am," Demon replies. He's in the van behind us with Cash, Axle, Viper, and Rage.

"Make sure none of the men leave the van without their masks."

"Will do," Demon's voice comes through again.

Knox hands us black masks. I grab mine from him with a shaky hand. "Leave them on till I say otherwise," he says.

Knox taps Reaper's shoulder. Reaper, who's driving, accelerates fast, making me slip further into my seat.

My pulse thrashes against my skin as I pull the mask over my head. My heart pounds on my ribcage like it's trying to break free. As we get to a clearing, lights glint from a mansion on a hillside. The mansion is surrounded by a vast wall.

"Are you sure that security is off, Twitch?" Knox asks.

"One hundred percent—I've got your back. Don't forget the electricity circuit on the right side of the house, if you want the electricity off. And ensure the generator isn't linked to the house."

The van veers off the road and drives up the hill, along the wall. Kane leans over and slides the van door open. Everything is tingling.

"Pass me the gun in the center console," Knox asks Reaper.

As I'm stepping out onto the ground, the other van pulls up behind us. I look up at the wall and see security cameras on top. I hope Twitch knows what he's doing.

Knox grips my arms. His eyes pierce mine. "Are you sure you want to come inside? You can wait here with Twitch."

"No, I want to come. I want to look her in the eye and find out why."

All the men stand around us waiting for instructions. Faint screamy music plays. One man has an earpiece in one of his ears. I peer at his eyes and glance down. The tattoos on his hands indicate it's Demon.

Knox's eyes land on Kane, and he steps toward him, places his hand on his shoulder, and squeezes it. "If you're thinking about going off by yourself or doing anything that can put any of us in danger, you can sit your ass back down in the car." The warning hangs heavy in the air.

"As long as you get me my answers," Kane replies through gritted teeth.

"Trust me to handle this."

Kane gives the slightest nod, so Knox hands him the gun.

"Are the guns necessary?" I ask.

Knox tilts his head an inch to the side. "We always carry them on us."

Viper and Cash get the ladder off the roof of the van, and Knox goes to Reaper's side and whispers something to him. Reaper looks at me while they're talking.

Reaper looks back at Knox and nods. We follow the men to the wall.

With the few lights on the property, I can see that it's a three-level mansion, modern in shape, dark, with large, black-tinted windows.

Knox turns to me. "Stay with Reaper." His eyes flick to Kane. "You are to go behind them. Stay with us. Don't go anywhere by yourself and do not shoot anyone unless it's necessary."

Adrenaline kicks in as they place the ladder against the wall. Knox is the first one to go over. I go to step forward, but Reaper gently tugs on my arm, holding me back.

"Demon is next, then Viper, me, then you." There is no negotiation in Reaper's tone.

I shuffle my feet, my heart beating in my ears. Demon travels up the rungs with ease, then Viper. My breathing is out of control, short and quick. Reaper is next. Then I move and grab the sides of the ladder.

Axle holds the ladder for me as I climb on shaky legs,

putting one foot above the other. As I get to the top, the house lights go off and we are plunged into darkness. At the top of the wall, the edging is wide enough that I can stand on it.

A light shines below. "Jump, I've got you," Reaper's voice rumbles. Nothing is stopping me from going inside, so I close my eyes and jump. I let out a breath of relief when I land in two arms and then my feet are placed on the ground.

I scan the yard, though I can't see much. The stars in the sky provide little light, but enough to see objects in front of me.

When the rest of the men get over the wall, we dash to Viper and Knox. Reaper is by my side as we move in a line and hurry toward the back of the house.

Demon moves ahead to the door, and when I shuffle to the side, I can see him picking the lock. The door opens with ease, making me wonder just how many times he has done it.

Before we step inside, Knox says, "The bedrooms are on the top level." Once in, I stay in the middle of the pack with Reaper and Kane while the others clear every room before we reach the stairs to the next level.

"We must separate. There's too much ground to cover, and we don't know how long the security will be disabled for. Cash, Rage, Axle, and Viper, you go through this level and let me know if there's anyone there. Afterward, all of you get out of here," Knox says to the group.

There's a round of grunts, but Viper leads them away and Knox directs us up another set of stairs. The sounds of boots against the steps makes my stomach twist.

Demon heads past us to go step in stride with Knox, both with their hands on their guns, which have flashlights attached to them. As we move down the hallway, I see bedrooms to the left and right.

Knox and Demon move ahead. I step toward them, but Reaper tells me and Kane, "Us three stay here."

Demon opens the first door wide, and Knox walks in with his gun pointed forward. "Clear," Knox says softly. After going through another bedroom, Demon and Knox move to either side of another door. Knox whispers, "This is the main bedroom." He looks at Demon. "You open the door," he mouths to him. "Three. Two. One."

Demon opens the door and they go inside. "Hands up! Hands up!" Knox booms.

I rush forward, but Reaper's got me by the vest. He reaches out for Kane, but Kane shoves past him until he's in the room with Knox and Demon.

There's a high-pitched scream. "Where's Misty?" Kane demands, his tone harsh.

"Please, please, let me go in, Reaper," I screech as adrenaline courses through me. Desperation of knowing who's in that room consumes me. I pull forward, but Reaper's grip keeps me in my spot.

A slap echoes. "What was that?" I'm on edge, listening intently.

Audrey and Kane walk out of the room, Knox's light shining on Audrey. She's wearing a white night gown and holds one hand over her heart as she breathes out heavily, wide eyed. "Let go of me!"

Demon and Knox walk out behind them.

"Where are you taking me? What's this about?" Audrey screeches.

Kane rips his mask off, then raises his gun, aiming it at Audrey. "Where is Misty?"

Horror flashes across Audrey's face. "Kane?" she whispers. Her shoulders fall. Then she looks at Knox. He takes his mask off. Her eyes dart to the bedroom they just came out of. "You didn't have to hurt him."

"Your bodyguard is only unconscious, but don't think we won't harm him if we need to," Knox threatens.

"Tell me now!" Kane's voice is deadly, making me think he might go through with it—he might kill Audrey.

Anger strikes me too. I yank the mask off my face and glare at her. "You saw Misty last, you lying bitch! Answer him!"

Tears line Audrey's eyes.

Footsteps sound behind us. It's the rest of the MC's men. Audrey takes a step back. Reaper's hand comes out in a stopping motion and the men pause.

"Have you got this?" Reaper asks Knox.

"All of you can go."

Reaper answers. "I'll wait outside. Do you want the electricity back on?"

"Yes," Knox replies.

Reaper walks to the men.

Demon points to the bedroom. "Do you want me to take the bodyguard?"

"No!" Audrey shrieks.

"I'll take him, if need be," Knox answers him.

Demon's shoulders sink.

I watch as the men walk down the hallway and then turn my attention back to Audrey. Silence crackles between us.

Knox shifts, turning. "Do I have to break some of the security guard's bones to get you to talk?" He steps toward the room.

"It was an accident. Misty and I fought for a gun, and it went off," Audrey blurts out. A burst of air escapes my lips.

"What did you just say? Are you saying she's dead?" Kane asks softly, sounding afraid of her answer.

Tears flood Audrey's face. She nods sharply.

The agony that flashes across Kane's face breaks my heart. The wound from Misty's disappearance has just been sliced open again. My head pounds, my heart aches, and my vision blurs.

"Tell us everything!" Kane screams at her. "Now!" He brings the gun closer to her, only an inch from her head.

Audrey swallows hard, her eyes on the floor. "Misty came over that day and was waiting for you," she says, making eye contact with Kane. "She told me she was pregnant with your baby. Could you imagine the scandal we would have had with her being pregnant, with you as the father? The both of you were too irresponsible and young. You could never have raised a child at that age."

His lip curls. "I didn't ask for your opinion. I asked what happened to her," he roars.

Audrey flinches. "I suggested that she have an abortion, but she refused, though she was ashamed of the baby and didn't want to disappoint her family and you," she says as she stares at Kane. "I thought there was one option left, and that was to give birth to the baby in secrecy and put it up for adoption. So, before you came home, I told Misty we had a holiday house she could stay at."

The pieces fall together. "Everything was a lie. You played everyone!"

She looks at me with tears and remorse in her eyes. "We ended up getting rid of Misty's phone and car. Misty and I came up with a plan that she supposedly came to break up with Kane and left because she needed some space but would be back. I was supposed to tell everyone that she told me instead, because Kane wasn't home, but I didn't say anything to anyone, and after that the lies kept on piling up."

"What did you do to Misty?" I ask, shocked.

"Misty ended up wanting to keep the baby and go home, but I couldn't let her expose everything we had done. Then, one night, she got her hands on the security guard's gun. Me and her fought over it, then the gun went off. It was an accident." She sobs harder, struggling to breathe.

Kane's hands shake while holding the gun. Audrey closes her eyes, ready to meet her maker.

Knox slowly raises his hand and puts the other over Kane's gun. "We have her. Don't do this. Now, put the gun down and let me notify Parker, our contact at the police station."

Kane shakes his head, pushing the gun into her forehead, making her let out a brief scream. "It's not enough," Kane yells, fat tears rolling down his face. "She'll get out. You know she has money and connections."

"No, she won't. Kidnapping and manslaughter—she will do time. Let her live . . . let her suffer."

Kane's eyes are trained on his mother. "She deserves to die," Kane reiterates.

"She does, but she also deserves to rot in a cell. Death will be an easy way out for her," Knox replies, desperately trying to stop Kane from doing something he'll regret.

Lights flick on. Kane's shoulders slump in defeat as Knox helps him lower the gun.

"Nanny."

I turn to the softly spoken voice, and nothing could have prepared me for what I see next.

BEST
FR—ENDS

TWENTY
DISCOVERY

Zara

A GIRL GLANCES BETWEEN EVERYONE. HER EYES RETURN TO Audrey. "Why is everyone being so loud? Nanny, why are you crying?"

Audrey rubs her eyes and her face. She clears her throat. "Everything is all right," she replies.

The girl walks toward us. When I get a better look at her, the wind is knocked out of me, as if I'm dreaming I'm on the merry-go-round. It's going round and round faster and faster, and all I see is Misty's face at that age, smiling back at me. The room spins. My knees hit the ground.

My world halts. Misty's face morphs into the girl's. She looks like Misty did when she was younger, except for Kane and Knox's whiskey-colored eyes. This is a dream. It can't be real. I didn't think she was alive.

"What's your name?" I ask her in a small voice.

"Avyanna."

"That's a beautiful and unusual name."

She peers up at Audrey. "Nanny said my mom gave it to me. It means strong and beautiful."

I breathe out a long breath at the mention of Misty. It's such a perfect and fitting name. I look up at Kane, who is frozen in place. He looks over every inch of her. His hands tremble, and tears fall.

I bring my eyes back to Avyanna. "I'm your auntie and he," I say as I glance at Kane, "is your father."

She peers back at Audrey for reassurance. She nods to Avyanna. "It's your dad."

Avyanna stills, her eyes darting between all of us. "It's okay," Audrey says softly. A slow smile paints Avyanna's face as she runs to Kane and leaps into his arms. He goes from frozen to melting into his daughter's embrace. He cradles her against his chest and kisses the top of her head as more tears stream down his cheeks.

Knox leans down to me and helps me stand on unsteady legs.

Kane keeps looking over Avyanna, checking that she's real, and then pulls her back into a tighter hug. She giggles. The sound makes my chest constrict.

When Kane puts Avyanna down, Knox steps toward her. He bends down until he's at her height. "I'm Knox, your uncle. Nice to meet you," he says as they shake hands.

She smiles. "I have an uncle too!" She peers up at Audrey. "Did you hear that, Nanny?"

She blinks furiously. "I did, dear," Audrey replies.

"Did you get to meet your mom?" I ask Avyanna.

She shakes her head and frowns. "Nanny said she went to heaven when I was a baby."

My heart splinters at her words, and it takes everything in me to contain myself and not lash out at Audrey. She stole so many moments from everyone. "I knew your mother. She was my best friend, and my sister."

Avyanna's eyes widen. "What was she like?"

"She would have been an exceptional mother to you. I'm sorry you didn't get to spend time with her. She looked out for me, and I always envied how strong she was." I grab a lock of Avyanna's hair and twist it between my fingers. "And you look just like her, but you have your dad's eyes."

"I'm going to call Parker," Knox says to me, then peers at Audrey. "Say your goodbyes now."

Audrey makes her way to Avyanna while Kane glowers at her. She bends down, grabbing Avyanna's hands. "I've got to go away for a while, so you're going to stay with your dad."

She frowns. "How long are you going away for?"

She sniffles, and when I glance at Audrey, she's crying. "I'm not too sure yet. But I will see you. Now you better go with your dad so you can get your bags packed."

Knox walks back. "The police are on their way."

"Show me to your room?" Kane asks Avyanna. She puts her hand in his and they wander down the hallway.

Knox lifts his walkie-talkie to his mouth. "Hey, you still there?"

"Yeah, man," Twitch replies.

"Police are on their way. You and Reaper get out of here, but pick us up in about half an hour. I don't want any of you here when the cops get here."

"Downstairs, now," Knox says to Audrey.

He follows closely behind her through the hallway and down the stairs and out the front door. Police sirens wail.

"This will be the last freedom you will have for a while," says Knox.

"I didn't mean to kill Misty. You have to believe me."

Knox chuckles darkly. "You were so obsessed with your image that you jeopardized any chance for Avyanna to have a mother in her life, and you've selfishly taken all those years away from your own son."

Blue-and-red lights flicker, and I watch as a sedan and two cop cars make their way to the mansion.

Dread slithers up, gripping my throat. I grab Audrey's arm. "Where's Misty buried?"

"There's a plaque in the backyard with her name on it. It's surrounded by flowers. Exactly the way Avyanna wanted it."

"We're ready!" I drop my arm and peek over Audrey's shoulder to see Kane and Avyanna walking toward us. With one hand Kane's dragging a large hot-pink suitcase with a large tote bag on top. He's holding Avyanna's hand with the other.

AFTER TALKING TO THE POLICE, WE DROP KANE AND AVYANNA off at Kane's house. As much as I want to spend time with her, the sun would be up soon and she should stay with Kane.

When we walk inside the clubhouse, all the men are awake and seated at the bar. Everyone stops talking and all eyes are on us, but it's me who speaks. "I'd like to thank everyone again. With your help, we could find answers that have been haunting our families for over ten years." There's a round of cheers and claps. "I'm both happy and sad to report that my sister had passed away, but her daughter Avyanna is alive and well and is with her father, Kane, now."

There are gasps and a mix of feelings on everyone's faces.

I peer back at Knox. "I'm going to go to bed. I'm exhausted. You can stay up with the men."

He shakes his head and links our fingers together. "I'm coming with you."

"Night, everyone," Knox calls out. Hand in hand, we go up the stairs and to Knox's room. Once inside, I pull the comforter back and sit on the edge of the bed. I take my sneakers off, then lie down.

Knox's phone rings. He pulls it out of his pocket, looks at the screen, then places it on the side table. "Who is it?"

"My uncle. I presume Audrey has called the family lawyer to represent her. I'm sure my uncle wants to know everything."

"Aren't you going to answer it?"

"I'll talk to him when we wake up." He kicks his shoes off and shuffles in next to me. He folds his arm over me, pulls my back flush against him, and covers my hand with his. "All I need now is you."

"You have me."

Forever . . . I have nothing to run from anymore. My life is here with Knox, Kane, Avyanna, and my parents. Soon we'll be faced with the heartbreaking duty of informing my parents about the tragic events that unfolded.

BEST
FRIENDS

TWENTY-ONE
UNTIL WE MEET AGAIN

Zara

TWO WEEKS HAVE PASSED SINCE THAT NIGHT. WE'VE GIVEN OUR statements to the police. Audrey is in jail being held without bail. Her security guard provided details of the kidnapping and confirmed Audrey's story for a lesser sentence.

I rub my leg, anxiousness taking hold. Kane is pacing in front of me, wearing marks into the carpet. Mom has a blank stare. She was always the one who had hope, even when I told her that Audrey said Misty had passed away. Mom refused to accept it.

There's a knock on the door. Knox goes to stand, but his dad, David, puts his hand out to stop him and stands instead. "No, son, I'll get it. You stay with Zara."

I give him a sad smile. He's been visiting all of us most days. I see the heavy burden that Audrey's actions have placed on all the men in the Hart family.

Officer Parker walks in with David. Kane halts when he sees him, and Parker gives us a tight smile.

"Well?" Kane asks, cutting to the chase.

Parker holds my stare as he brings his hand out to me and places a necklace into my palm, the best friend one Misty and I shared. A painful scream tears from Mom's throat. Dad is by her side, holding her.

"No . . . no . . . no. Not my baby," she sobs.

Knox wraps me in his arms.

"We found this with the body. Do you recognize it?" Parker asks.

I nod briefly, unable to talk because of the constriction in my throat.

"What is it?" Kane asks.

I clear my throat and show him the necklace. "It was hers," I whisper. I bring hers against my own, showing how the two parts link to form a single heart.

Kane's body droops as he sits back down, his head in his hands. David squeezes Kane's shoulders as tears fall down his face.

"We'll confirm her identity with you once the DNA results come in."

"Thank you." Knox speaks for all of us.

"It's okay. I can see myself out."

"Has there been an update about the charges laid against Audrey?" I ask Parker before he leaves.

"There's a strong legal case. She's facing charges for murder, kidnapping, and the imprisonment of Avyanna."

So she should.

"Thank you."

After he leaves, I turn to my mom and put my arm around her. "We still have a piece of Misty with us. Avyanna is our little miracle," I say out loud to everyone, hoping to ease their pain.

Everything is a blur until we receive the results confirming that the body is indeed Misty's. We find the perfect cemetery for her close by, one overlooking the water.

A feeling of peace has cloaked me since finding the truth. Kane and Mom are still struggling, but having Avyanna gives them something to be grateful for, even under these circumstances.

When we lay her to rest, after everyone has said goodbye, I stay behind. I slowly walk over and place a single sunflower on her casket as I smile down at her. "You finally got the send-off you deserved," I say as I touch the smooth-grained wood of the casket. "I've missed you so much. It's hard to believe it's been so long since you've been gone. I wish you were here, but I know you're smiling down at us."

I release a ragged breath. "I'll try my best to help Kane raise your beautiful daughter. I hope we make you proud. She's been in my life for a short while, but I don't know what life would be like without her in it."

A little giggle escapes me. "She looks exactly like you, and I'm sure you're amused that she has your sass and attitude already and has her daddy and grandparents wrapped around her little finger. No one can say no to her because she deserves the world . . . and so much more."

I peer over at Knox. He's too far away to hear me, but he's still watching closely—always watching me. "I want you to know that I'm happy with Knox. He is everything I ever needed. He loves me for me, even with all my battle scars."

I kiss my fingers and press them to the casket. "Best friends forever," I whisper. "Until we meet again."

NEW BEGINNINGS

Three months later

Zara

Knox and I left a couple of days after the funeral to get my belongings from my home in the city. I spoke to my manager to hand in my resignation. It was sad leaving her and my colleagues—and the women's shelter where I put my heart and soul into helping other people, though I know it's in good hands.

As I'm tossing the salad, I gaze at the newest members of my family. I'm blown away every day by how much Avyanna reminds me of Misty, even though they never truly met.

"How's that mac and cheese coming along, Avyanna?" Ava asks as she peeks into the oven.

Avyanna spoons a small scoop into her mouth, then her lips curve into a blinding smile. "Yum!"

"Don't put the spoon back in. Put it in the sink." My words hurry out before she contaminates the food.

"I saw that!" Twitch grumbles. He looks at Ava with one brow raised. "How come she gets to eat it?"

Ava waves him off. "She's a child. You're a grown adult. She can try it."

"Is he really an adult, though? He acts like a child." Elena's voice is full of amusement.

Axle points a finger at Twitch. "Ha! Take that!"

Elena whips around to face Axle. "Don't you talk. You are just as bad as him, if not worse."

Twitch's lips rise into a victorious smile as he looks at Axle with mocking eyes.

"Babe, me and you," Axle says as his finger flicks between the two of them, "are supposed to be a team and ahh . . . you aren't pulling your weight."

Ava opens the oven, steam rises. She uses tea towels to pull out a huge chicken with baked vegetables. The smell saturates the air, making my stomach grumble.

I look at Ava. "Salad's done. Do you want cling film over it?"

"Yes, please," Ava replies.

Reaper walks into the busy kitchen from the living room. "Would you like some help?"

Ava nods. "Ham is in the fridge, and I need someone to take the cookies." She tilts her head toward the large container with the blue lid on the counter.

Knox stands from the stool. "On it."

"Twitch, can you take the fried rice that's beside me?"

"Yep," Twitch answers.

"This is a test run . . . I hope everyone likes it and that it's good enough," Ava says, then nibbles on her bottom lip.

My eyes tear up. "Of course they will. You'll never grasp

how much they will appreciate it. To have a people be there for them means the world."

She tilts her head back and blinks furiously, then she scans the room, looking at all of us. "I know exactly what that feels like."

I look around at everyone, at the women and men who have been by our sides and offered their assistance and support. "I know too," I answer.

"So what are we doing again?" Avyanna asks, though her eyes are still locked onto the mac and cheese.

"It's a surprise," I blurt out, not wanting to give anything away. She doesn't know. Hell, Mom and Dad and Kane don't know. We have been good at keeping this secret from them. Avyanna heard us talking about cooking food for a surprise occasion, so she wanted to help.

"Are the guys finished and ready for everyone to see? Knox, can you call them to check?"

He shoots me a smile, and it lessens the nervousness. "They will be fine. Now, are we ready to go?"

"Yes," I answer, dying to see what the place looks like finished.

We pile into the vans and truck.

Fifteen minutes later, I pull up to a redbrick hall that the Crown family owned but gave to us because we needed a place. The van's side door slides across, and I'm out first, with a large bowl of salad in hand.

"It's perfect." I rush forward, goose bumps traveling across my skin. The front lawn is a lush green, with a cream-colored paved path to the entrance door. On the side is a blanket covering what I know to be a large plaque that says "Misty's Safe Haven."

After we buried Misty, I was determined to ensure that her death wasn't in vain. I wanted to help others who are going through traumatic experiences. With the help of family and friends, I created a charity called Misty's Safe Haven.

The charity will also have a hotline women and children can call if they feel they are in danger. The Harts and the MC have offered to assist by removing the victims from the situation and bringing them to the charity, which will provide free meals, shelter, and other necessities.

After my mom, dad, and Kane see it, I plan to contact local professionals like counselors and lawyers who can help victims get back on their feet. I've managed a shelter before, so I can use my skills and assist with getting the victims jobs and accommodation.

Ava has been cooking up ridiculous amounts of food, ensuring she masters every dish before the shelter opens. I'm so proud of what we've achieved, and I couldn't have done it without the help of the MC.

Viper greets me at the door. He gives me one of his easy smiles. He reaches out and grasps the salad. "I'll take that. Come check it out. Turned out better than I imagined."

I want to . . . so bad. "No, I want it to be a surprise with Mom, Dad, and Kane."

"How long till they get here?"

"Shouldn't be long."

Seeing the smiles and excitement radiating from the men truly touches my soul and warms my heart. Allowing them to help, to be a part of something that's important and special, has brought out how amazing this group really is. I helped with the layout of the shelter and ordered what we needed, but they have spent late nights renovating, painting, and putting furniture and beds together.

"Can I tell you one thing?" He's bursting at the seams like a little child at Christmas.

I chuckle at his excitement. "Okay, what?"

"We've put together a playground for the kids," he blurts

out. "Demon has outdone himself. The kids are going to love it." He hurries off.

I step outside and wait on the front lawn for everyone to walk inside. I hear gasps and squeals. I shuffle from one foot to the other, holding myself back from going inside.

I squint as a familiar car turns up the street. I dash to the door. "Everyone, they are here! Quick, quick!" I yell.

I hear footsteps as I hurry back to the grass. The car pulls up to the curb in front of me and I nervously wait until they get out.

David knows about it, so I've had him distracting them this morning. He gives me a knowing smile. Mom, Dad, and Kane step out of the car looking confused. Avyanna darts out to Kane.

I wipe my clammy hands on my jeans before I step closer to Mom and kiss her cheek. "I've got a surprise for the three of you." I move to the front of the hall and usher them over until they are close. "Welcome to . . ." I pull the blanket down, and as it falls, it reveals a silver plaque engraved with "Misty's Safe Haven."

Mom's shaky hands go to her mouth as Dad's lip trembles.

"It's a safe haven for women and children where we'll provide them with the resources they need to get their lives back on track."

It's Dad who rushes to me and hugs me tight. "I'm so very proud of you," he whispers into my ear. He sniffles and pulls back, wiping his now glassy eyes.

"That's Mom's name," Avyanna says as she inspects it. She steps closer, looking at the smaller writing at the bottom. "In loving memory of Misty Pratt, a sister, a daughter, a mother, and a best friend. Her life a beautiful memory that will never be forgotten," she reads out, then peers up at me. "This is for Mom?"

"Yes, we created this to honor her." Maybe, if Misty had something like this to turn to, to get anonymous advice or help, things would have been different.

Viper appears. "Everything is ready."

"Thank you," I reply.

"Dad, Dad," Avyanna says. "Are you okay? Don't cry." She wraps her arms around her dad.

He mouths "Thank you" to me. I smile back, glad that they're happy.

I grasp Mom's hand in mine. "Let's take the tour. Viper, did you want to do the honors?"

His face, if possible, brightens more. He gestures broadly at the center. "Welcome, follow me . . ."

BEST
FRIENDS

TWENTY-THREE
THE BRIGHTEST STAR

Eight months later

Zara

It's Misty's anniversary again, and it's bittersweet. We go to visit her often, but today is different. I walk into the house with a bunch of bright-yellow sunflowers and put my keys and bag down on the table by the entrance.

This anniversary differs from others. No more lies, no more nightmares, no more cuts. When she visits me in my dreams, I still see her face and her beautiful blond hair and zest for life, which I see in her daughter too.

When I go out into the backyard, the sight before me makes me laugh. Viper and Avyanna are dancing to "You Can Do It" by Ice Cube. They roll their bodies from left to right in unison with the lyrics and I smile in amusement, thinking Misty would do the same with them if she were here.

When Avyanna looks up at me, she beams. "Viper's teaching me the dance."

"Is he now?" I dare a peek at Kane, who rolls his eyes, but there's a smirk on his lips.

"She has potential," Viper chimes in.

"Since when are you a dance teacher?" Axle yells out.

Noting the swearing and offensive language of the song, I ask, "Where can I change the music?"

"It's connected to my phone," Twitch answers, phone in hand.

"Can you change it . . . to something more appropriate," I say as I look at Avyanna.

Viper scoffs. "Oh please, she hears swearing all the time."

I try my best to stifle a laugh while two arms come around me, hugging me and pulling me into a broad chest. I turn to see Knox giving me one of his devastating smiles.

"He has a point," he says into my ear.

Avyanna runs to me and puts her arms around my waist so that I'm sandwiched between the two of them. I have to lift the flowers above Avyanna's head so they don't get crushed.

"It's a good song, Aunty Zara." I smile back at Avyanna as her eyes widen at the flowers. "Are those for Mom?" she asks.

"They sure are."

"When are we going?"

"Now, because we're going to see your mom first and then we're going to Crown Village Amusement Park."

"Yes!" she says, excited. "Can I come back here afterward?"

Kane walks to us and peers down at Avyanna. "We'll be back tomorrow for lunch. Nan and Pop will be here as well."

Knox, Avyanna, Kane, and I go together to Misty's grave before setting out for the amusement park.

Avyanna gets to go on her mom's favorite rides, which are now her favorite rides too—no surprises there. Now that I know the truth and have accepted it, I don't look for Misty in the crowds anymore.

We stay for hours, sharing stories with Avyanna about her mother, one being the time Misty cheekily smashed the ice cream in Kane's face. I smile at all the precious memories we share. No one can take those away from us.

After we get off the bumper cars, Kane says, "We'd better get going."

Avyanna groans, making me chuckle.

"We can come back another time," Kane tells her.

"Fine," she grumbles. He has got his hands full with her. Kane shakes his head with a smile.

A hand tugs on my wrist. I peer back at Knox. He drops to one knee.

I gasp as my heartbeat quickens. He looks up at me with that smile that's reserved for me. He opens the navy case to reveal an elegant engagement ring with a pear-shaped diamond stone.

"Zara, I know what it's like to live without you, and I could never do that again. You are everything to me, and I'm nothing without you. As you know, life is short, and I can't wait another second without us being bound in every way possible. Be my wife, and I promise to make you happy for the rest of your life."

"Yes, of course," I answer with a shaky voice.

His whole face transforms into sheer happiness. I'm holding back tears.

Knox stands and puts the ring on my finger. He holds my face in his hands as he bends down and touches his lips to mine in a lingering kiss.

"I love you so much," he says, his eyes flashing with so many emotions.

"I love you too," I whisper back.

Kane comes over to us. "Congratulations! You two deserve to be happy."

My eyes glisten. "So do you," I say back to him.

Kane pats Knox on the back.

Avyanna jumps to me, all excited, her mother's best-friends necklace bouncing from side to side around her neck. She looks at my ring. "That's really pretty."

"It is," I answer.

We walk back to the car. The night is dark, apart from the moon lighting up the sky and the stars shining brightly. Avyanna skips up to me and puts her hand in mine. I look down at her and notice she's looking up at the stars.

"Which one do you think is Mommy?" she asks.

I close my eyes briefly, then look at Kane as he steps up to Avyanna and takes her other hand in his.

"The brightest star in the sky, baby girl."

AFTER WE GET BACK TO THE CLUBHOUSE, I WALK THROUGH THE front door, but I don't get far as Elena and Ava dive on me, grabbing my hand.

"Oh, it's beautiful," Ava says and kisses my cheek. "Congratulations!"

Elena gives me a tight hug. "Congratulations."

My eyes flick between the two of them. "How do you know already?"

"Bomber told Reaper and Viper. Viper told Axle." Elena cringes. "And Axle told everyone."

As we walk further inside, Cash, Rage, Reaper, and Twitch crowd around Bomber. I hear a round of congratulations coming from them.

Axle makes his way to me and pulls me into his arms. "Congratulations and good luck."

I pull back with a smirk. "What do you mean good luck?"

"Having to deal with that cranky bastard for the rest of your life."

I laugh out loud.

Viper's next. He puts his arms around my shoulders. "Congrats!" He peers up at the men. "Bomber." Knox turns to him. "I shotgun organizing the bachelor party!"

"Fuck yeah!" Axle is the first to yell out. Elena glares at him. "Oh . . . I meant boooo!"

"No strippers!" Elena warns sternly.

"I'm not having strippers," Knox tells Elena. She looks relieved. I feel a bit of relief as well.

"We will have a joint party. There's no need for a bachelorette party," says Knox.

Viper chuckles, then peers down at me. "He just doesn't want *you* to have any strippers."

"You're boring, Knox!" Viper yells out in amusement. "Wait . . . will Bomber's cousin be invited?" Viper asks me.

"Yes," I reply, knowing that they will want to be there.

"Can you introduce me to Sophie?" he asks softly, so that only I can hear.

"Sure," I reply with a grin. He doesn't know what he's in for.

BEST
FRIENDS

TWENTY-FOUR
PEACE

Zara

"Hey, Mom." I smile brightly as she walks into my arms. When we pull back, I lift my hand up.

She grasps my hand and her mouth gapes open. "He didn't!"

I giggle. "He did!"

"John, your daughter's getting married."

Dad shakes Knox's hand and smiles. "That's wonderful news." Dad steps to me and leans in, giving me a kiss on the cheek.

"Follow me inside. Everyone is out the back," I say to them.

"There's quite a few people here," Mom points out as she looks at the parked motorcycles and cars.

"No, not really. Don't forget that a lot of people live here."

When we step inside, her eyes widen. She walks slowly as she inspects the clubhouse. "Are you two going to buy your own house now?"

I shake my head. "In the future . . . I actually enjoy living here. It's like an extended home."

When Mom moves to where all the men's police mug shots are displayed on the wall, she clicks her tongue. "Knox Hart." She emphasizes both his names. "What did you do?"

Knox puts his hands on her back, ushering her toward the rear of the house. "Oh, look, it's Elena," he says.

"Nice save," I mutter under my breath to Knox.

Mom throws her arms around Elena, and Elena hugs her back with a huge grin. "Mrs. Pratt, it's so good to see you again."

"You too, and please call me Helen." Seeing how well my parents get along with the ol' ladies and all the men from the MC makes me happy because I can have everyone together at once.

Ava comes running in through the back door and past us with her hands covering her mouth. My eyes flick back to Mom and Dad. "Kane and Avyanna are outside. You go sit. I'll check on Ava."

I follow Elena, and we rush to her. Ava's bent over the toilet, vomiting. I cringe at the sound of it, but also feel bad for her.

"Are you okay?" Elena asks. "Did you want me to go get Milly?"

Ava stands and presses the flush button. "No, I'm fine, really."

I know the signs. "You're pregnant!"

Elena squeals. Ava goes bright red. Elena points her finger at Ava. "You are!"

"We only found out a couple of days ago. Please keep it quiet . . . Reaper and I weren't going to tell anyone until I safely passed the twelve-week mark."

Elena squeals again and jumps up and down on the spot. I

grab Ava, giving her a tight hug. "I'm so excited for the two of you."

"I can't believe it. I'm going to be an aunty. I can't wait to go baby shopping!" Elena beams.

Ava's eyes stretch wide. "Shhh! No one can find out," she whispers. "With my endometriosis, I'm worried something bad could happen."

Elena raises her hands. "I'm sure everything is going to be fine. I won't say anything. I promise."

"I won't say anything either," I tell Ava. My heart fills with joy at the thought of her having a baby. She's such a loving person, she will be the perfect mother.

When we step outside, there's music playing in the background, but by the table there's chatter and laughter. As I take my seat beside Knox, his lips curve up into an affectionate smile, making my heart strum. He folds his hand over mine and I lean into him. I'm the one who gets to see every side of him . . . his love . . . his compassion . . . his devotion.

Reaper's frowning. He and Ava talk in hushed tones. I peer around the table of friends and family and see only a few people I don't know. "Who's the attractive woman sitting next to Twitch?"

The woman's head falls back as she laughs, her hand going to Twitch's leg.

"Reaper's sister, Milly. She's a doctor."

Twitch smiles back at her. They hold eye contact.

"Are they together?"

"No."

I look up at Knox. "They look like they're a couple."

Knox's shakes his head. "It's not going to happen. It's Reaper's sister. They just flirt."

I keep my mouth closed, but I have a feeling, by the way they are looking at each other, it might be more than just *friends.*

"Oh dear lord," Mom calls out in a high-pitched voice. She's sitting on the other side of me. Her eyes are on Conan.

"He's friendly, Mom."

She sits up straighter in her chair. "He certainly doesn't look like it." Conan's sitting next to the barbecue, massive strands of drool hanging from both sides of his mouth. Avyanna runs to Conan and Mom yells "No!" but Avyanna doesn't listen and pats Conan on the head.

"See, Nan, he's a friendly dog." Conan licks her hand and she giggles.

Mom's shoulders fall in relief and an adoring smile lights up her face as she watches Avyanna. As I peek around the table, Kane and Knox share the same smile as Mom, and my chest could burst from happiness.

Knox

Later that night

"Are you sure about this?" I ask Kane, one more time, allowing him the opportunity to back out, because once it's done, he can't come back from this.

Kane's lips press into a hard line. "I've never been so sure about anything in my life. Burn it down to the ground."

I stare at Audrey's mansion that held Avyanna and Misty captive. I press the detonator and brace for impact. The blast shoots bright yellow flames and scatters debris through the sky. A rush of air hits my face. We're far enough away to not be hit by the explosion. The destruction of the structure provides an odd feeling of satisfaction, enjoyment even, that the house that held years of pain and secrets is gone forever.

I pull the burner phone from my back pocket, press the

number for Harrison—my cousin who's a firefighter—and bring the phone to my face.

"Hello," he answers in a croaky voice.

"You didn't hear it from me, but Audrey's place just exploded."

There's shuffling. "You just blew up her house?"

I chuckle. "Yeah, we did."

There's a breath. "Fuck, man . . . Honestly, I don't blame you. House of horrors. Is it just the house or has it started fires outside the walls?"

"Not that I can see."

"We're on our way," he says.

"Focus on ensuring the fire doesn't extend to outside the home, but let the house burn for a while. We want nothing to be left there."

"I'll do my best," he answers.

Kane, Zara, and I get into the van and drive away. I watch in the side mirror as the flames dance in the sky's darkness.

I place my hand on top of hers. She looks at me and smiles. I'm in awe of her fearlessness and passion to help others. Hell, she brought the men in our MC closer together. Like being in the military, we are honored to help women and children in the community and are once again proud of ourselves and what we have accomplished.

"This is what freedom feels like," Zara says in the passenger seat next to me.

I glance at her; she has a small smile. I know she's referring to Audrey's house—the last painful piece of the past has been eliminated—but for me, it's not just that. My freedom comes from Zara returning to me. She broke the chains that had stopped me from living.

Zara is the very essence of my being, the life that runs through my veins, the heartbeat of my existence, and the one who completes me in every way.

The end.

If you want to see Zara and Knox's celebratory combined bachelorette and bachelor party, view the sneak peek of Viper.

Did you want to go into the draw to win a *free paperback*? Sign up for my mailing list. Simply opening my newsletter emails enters you to win any paperback.

If you love my books, please leave a *review* or *rating* on your purchased retailer or your favorite platform. It encourages other readers to take a chance on me. It truly makes a difference and provides crucial feedback.

SNEAK PEEK AT VIPER

Viper

"Shots! Shots! Shots!" Axle, my MC brother, hollers as he walks toward us with a tray of shots.

I rub my hands together. "Fuck yeah!" I reply enthusiastically. My mission is celebrating Bomber and Zara's soon-to-be marriage, but I also want to sleep with Bomber's cousin Sophie. I don't want to get too drunk because if I can get her in the sheets, I want to remember every curve of her body, her taste, her scent—everything about her. I'm aware I'll be lucky to ever sleep with someone as classy as her again.

I've caught a glimpse of Sophie a few times, while she's been back. If it were a different woman, I would have at least chatted her up. I shake my head. Well… tonight's my chance.

When I pick up the overfilled shot glass, the liquid trickles down and onto my hand. I wait until everyone has a shot in their hand, and then I raise mine. "To Bomber and Zara," I yell.

Everyone cheers, "To Bomber and Zara."

We clink our shot glasses together, then I toss the shot

down my throat, feeling the burn. I'm left with a sweet taste in my mouth, but I enjoy it better than the last shot.

"What's the name of that one?" I ask Axle, having to raise my voice over the music.

His grin widens. "Wet pusssyyyyyy," he replies, making me laugh.

"No wonder I like the taste of it then," I say with a wink, then turn my attention to Ava. "Aren't you having any shots tonight?" She hasn't touched one that's been brought out.

Her eyes widen, but then she smiles. "No, thank you. I'm happy with my cocktail."

My brows lift. I bet it's a mocktail. I peer at her, then Reaper, who is her partner and the president of the MC. He subtly shakes his head at me, as in telling me to leave the topic. How stupid do they think I am? She's pregnant. I have no doubt about it. I'm patiently waiting for them to tell everyone.

Alec did an awesome job organizing Bomber and Zara's party. We got VIP access to this exclusive nightclub called Envy, so we didn't have to line up, and he got us a VIP table. But the best part is Alec set up a tab, so we don't have to pay for a drink all night.

The second floor is classier. Everything from the furniture to the lighting to the VIP bar. I settle back in my seat. I'm stoked that the sweet butts didn't come. Candy is a cool chick and all… but she's getting way too clingy. We have sex, that's it. I'm not interested in anything more. Having casual sex with her is convenient. I've told her time and time again what the deal is between us.

I lean over, putting my empty glass on the table. I peer around at the couples surrounding me. It feels like everyone is settling down. Axle and Elena, Reaper and Ava, now Bomber and Zara. The men will be attached to the women's hips tonight, never allowing them to go too far away. Possessive psychos. Though I don't blame them—I'd trust no man outside the club.

There's a twinge of jealousy I haven't experienced before. Seeing all the couples together and how well everyone gets along has me wondering if I want more than just hookups. I clear my throat... I can't believe that crossed my mind. Bomber and Zara's engagement and their promise of a happily ever after is messing with my head.

There's me, Twitch, Demon, Cash, and Rage, the last men standing, though I'm sure someone will be next. Twitch might sleep with Mercedez, one of the MC's sweet butts, but he's not interested in a relationship with her. And as much as he pines over Reaper's sister, Milly, he's got no chance. Rage is in his early twenties, still too young for anything serious, and I could laugh at Demon ever getting a woman. Perhaps it will be Cash, but according to the men, he still hasn't moved on from his past relationship.

I walk by our table and to the balcony that leads over to the first floor. The lights are dim where we are, with different colored flashing lights coming from the main stage. My shoulders move to the beat of techno music. Steve Aoki is killing it tonight. The first level is packed with people dancing.

There's a squeal, so I turn to see Zara standing, hugging Sophie. Harrison, Alec, and Lawson are off to the side, shaking hands with the MC men. Their family is beyond wealthy—like generational, old-money wealthy. Sophie looks incredible in a red dress that shows off her long legs. As I turn my gaze to the side to get a better sight of her, the slit in her dress reveals the creamy skin of her thigh. She should model for Victoria's Secret because she's an absolute bombshell.

I lean back on the edge of the balcony, drinking her in. I first saw her at Zara's sister's vigil, and I've never been so taken by a woman. I couldn't even go and talk to her, so I sussed her out, asking Zara and Bomber to give me the lowdown. Sophie used to be close to them when they were young, but they haven't kept in touch since she finished school, then moved away to New York.

Sophie is devoted. Coming home when her family and friends need her. She had a career on a silver platter because of all the businesses her family owns but moved away instead to pursue her own dreams. Sophie isn't just a beauty, she seems to be so much more, and that has piqued my interest. I've never wanted to spend more than one wild night with a woman, but I want to get to know her.

That we do business with her father should be reason not to go there because it could cause problems, but right now I'm living in the present. I can worry about all the other nonsense later.

When the men have shaken Bomber's cousins' hands, I step forward. I grasp Alec's hand in a firm handshake. He's a nice guy and all, but he looks like a tool being in a club with a suit on… though maybe that's his game. Showing women that he's loaded, because the Crowns are the richest people I've ever met.

Lawson's next, and we shake hands. "Hey," I say to him. He's a sexy son of a bitch, I'll give him that. My eyes drift over the family. They all are a good-looking bunch.

I pull back on seeing Harrison. His smile is wide. "Hey, man, how are you doing?" I ask him. He always says hi to me even though we don't know him well. He's dressed in a casual shirt and jeans, like the rest of us.

"Awesome… now." He glances around the club. "I haven't been back to Vegas in so long."

"I haven't either. The clubs are insane," I reply. I'm used to the parties back home in the MC clubhouse or at our local bar.

Harrison looks around, then tilts his head. "I'm going to the bar; do you want anything?"

I nod. "A beer, thanks."

"What type?"

"Anything will do."

He nods, then makes his way over to the bar as Sophie walks over to me. My pulse thrums. I scold myself for acting like a pussy. I can't stop my eyes from wandering down her breasts to the curve of her hips, to those long legs that I hope to be spreading tonight.

"Viper, is it?" she says, and I like the way my name rolls off her tongue a little too much. I'm getting a semi.

I inch back, giving her an indecent grin. "Sure is, darlin'."

I swear to God, I saw her mouth the word "delicious," but with the damn music up so loud, I can't hear shit. She pulls me in for a hug, which startles me for a second, but then I hug her back, appreciating her body against mine.

I take a deep breath and say, "You smell heavenly…" Mouth-watering and appetizing.

She leans back, giving me a seductive smile. "So do you… like coconut and lime."

Now I have a raging hard-on. She's giving me the eyes already, and I just met her. "Do you come to Vegas often?" I ask.

"No, but I'm in the clubbing scene," she says as she peers down at the crowd.

"It's a pretty good setup here," I say.

She arches a perfectly shaped brow. "Mine's better."

"Yours? What do you mean?"

She grins. "I own a club in New York."

I knew she left Crown Village for her modeling career, but I didn't know she owned a club. Beauty and brains. What a dangerous combination. "Businesswoman, hey… I'm impressed." She gives me a funny look I can't quite make out. "You model too, don't you?"

"Yes, but I'm not doing as many shows anymore. I want to focus on running my club."

"Fair enough." A successful, sexy, rich woman would intimidate most men. Not me—I think running a business just makes her more appealing. It's a nice change to hang out with a woman who's driven and motivated to do something with her life. I want to know everything about her and what makes her tick.

"What do you do?" she asks.

I point to the patch on my vest. "Vice president of the best motorcycle club in the US."

She smiles. "I know that, but what else do you do as a job?"

My shoulders tense. Her father, Garrett, and brother Alec know we grow, distribute, and sell large amounts of pot and aren't licensed. Hell, they said we could. Nothing goes on in the town without her father's say-so, but I don't know how much she knows, so I decide to talk about the charity.

"We help with Zara's charity, at the women and children's safe house."

Her face lights up. "It's unbelievable. Zara has done such a good job. After everything she's been through, she's turned a devastating outcome into something positive. So… what's your role in it?"

"We renovated the property and building where the charity houses the women and children. We help the victims, like picking them up and taking them away from dangerous situations they're in and bringing them to the charity." I think back to the frightened woman and children we picked up last week. "It's really brought the club together, everyone working together to help others. We're honored to assist, and the town's response to us has been positive." People now smile and praise us for helping rather than fearing us.

She steps closer to me and searches my eyes. "You're doing such a great job. I'm proud of you and everyone who's helped Zara."

She's proud of me? I don't think anyone has said that to me before. I give her one of my panty-dropping smiles.

She lifts her hands and grabs each side of my leather cut. "You look sexy in leather."

I'm the one who's supposed to be dishing out compliments. Maybe… just maybe… I'm in over my head with her.

I slip my arms out of my cut and hold it out for her, and without hesitation, she slides the leather vest on over her red dress. My mouth goes dry. Fuck meeeeeee! "Hmm… Temptress, you look better." My voice is husky and my hard-on is achingly uncomfortable against my jeans. An ol' lady property patch with my name on it would be even better.

I glance at the men to see if anyone noticed. Bomber's shaking his head at me and Axle's jaw is gaping. We don't let just anyone wear our club colors. No man outside the MC is allowed to wear our patch, and only the women we're serious about—our ol' ladies—get to wear a property patch with their man's name on it. By letting Sophie wear my cut, I know Axle is going to give me shit later for it.

I lean toward Sophie, pulling her blond wavy hair from under my cut and allowing it to fall down her back, while she gives me a slow once-over.

Harrison appears next to us and hands me my beer. "Thanks," I say, wishing I hadn't asked for it now.

"Where's my drink?" Sophie asks Harrison.

"Sorry, sis, you should have told me beforehand."

"Well… I might go over and order a cocktail. I'll be back soon," she says as she makes her way over to the bar, swaying those sexy hips. I stare at her, captivated.

Harrison's laugh brings my eyes back to him. "I almost feel bad for you."

I frown. "What do you mean?"

"It looks like Sophie's got her eye on you."

I chuckle. "I'm stoked with that." I peek at her again. She's at the bar and is flanked by a man on either side, undoubtedly trying to buy her a drink. Annoyance flares up inside of me. She's *mine* for tonight.

"I thought you were a one-night-stand type of guy."

I am, apart from Candy. "Why do you say that?" I ask.

"Well… you're looking at my sister like you want to be her knight in shining armor. Sophie can more than handle herself with men, but proceed with caution. Every man has wanted to bang her, and after one night, every one of them has wanted more from her. But she doesn't have any more to give, and if she sees you getting jealous or needy"—he looks at her, then at me, and I assume he means the way I'm acting now—"she will run. She's a player."

"What makes you think I want anything other than sex?"

He mocks me with his laughter.

"What?" I ask him.

"She's wearing your cut. She's already got you by the balls."

I chuckle but don't reply because Sophie comes over to us.

She tugs at my arm. "Come have a shot with me."

I smile back at her. "Sure, darlin'."

Harrison gives me an I-told-you-so grin.

I follow Sophie to the bar, where the barman ignores all the other patrons only talking to Sophie. "Your cocktail is being made now." He tilts his head to the lady mixing a blue drink in a fancy glass beside him. "Do you want anything else?" he asks, then licks his lips, his eyes flicking to her breasts, then back to her face.

I itch to say something, but I want Sophie in my bed badly, so I don't want to screw it up.

She gives him a naughty smile. "Two tequila shots, please." The man pulls out the shot glasses, pours the clear liquid into them, and puts the glasses in front of us. "Can we have lime and salt?" she asks. The barman obliges.

"Give me your hand," my little temptress demands. I follow her command. She dips her fingers into a drink and dabs tequila on the part of my hand between my thumb and index finger.

I watch as she shakes salt onto my wet skin. *She's not, is she...* Sophie bends down and runs her soft tongue along the edge of my hand, taking the salt with her, then she tosses her drink back. The movement is erotic.

Sophie places the lime between my lips, making my heart pound. She leans toward me, and her mouth presses against mine as she sucks the lime. My mouth waters—it's intoxicating. She seductively licks her lips. I swiftly down my shot, feeling the warmth of the alcohol, but my attention stays fixed on Sophie.

The barwoman places the cocktail in front of her. "Can I have two more tequila shots?" I ask. She gives me the once-over and then a flirty smile, so I smile back. As soon as the barwoman pours one shot, I take Sophie's hand in mine, dab my fingers into the liquid and dampen her hand, then shake the salt. My body hums in anticipation.

I bring her hand to my lips, and sensually lick the salt while maintaining eye contact. I delight in watching her eyes heat and those luscious lips part. I bring the glass to my lips and finish the shot, but instead of the lime, my hand goes to Sophie's chin. I lean down, sealing my mouth over hers. Sophie's lips are soft. I apply a gentle pressure to begin with and she kisses me back. As my tongue dips inside, I taste her with long, leisurely licks.

Her hands rise, looping over my shoulders until she's running her fingers through my hair. My heartbeat is surging as the kiss deepens. I press my lips against hers harder but try to rein in my wild passion. My hands slip to her hips, then the curve of her ass. The club evaporates, and all that's left is us. I break the kiss, then yank her hips toward mine. I slowly grind my pelvis against hers so that she can feel my hard-on.

Hunger burns in her eyes, proof that I'm not the only one who's turned on. I lean over and run my nose up her throat to her ear, noticing her breathing quicken. I place two kisses on her neck. "I can't wait to fuck you," I tell her, my voice rough.

She squirms. Goosebumps travel along her arms. *She likes the dirty talk.* My fingers dig into her sides. I want her now… to explore every inch of her. She slips her hand between us and grabs my dick through my jeans. I jerk and a hiss escapes me. She slowly rubs up and down, making my eyes roll back.

She bites down on her plump red bottom lip. "I'm ready for round one now," she purrs, and I let out a drawn-out groan. No shyness… just a woman who knows what she wants. I want to brand my name on her pretty little flesh and keep her all for myself.

"Four more shots of tequila," I say to the bartender. I'm already having fun with her. I don't want this night to end. With the two of us drunk together, the night is going to be wild.

I can't believe a man hasn't put a ring on her finger yet. She's the ultimate catch. I wonder what it would take for her to stay at the clubhouse with me and get to know me. Hell, if given the chance, I could show her I'm a decent guy and maybe, just maybe, I'd be worthy.

Grab your copy of <u>Viper</u> now.

RESOURCES

One Australian dollar of every paperback book purchase from Bianca's website will go to the LifeLine charity.

If you are struggling with your mental health, contact Life-Line. LifeLine is available in many countries and offers help for people experiencing emotional distress. They provide confidential crisis support, and in most instances, you can call, chat online, or text.

Please visit https://lifeline-intl.com/our-network/ for more information.

If you are seeking help with a drinking problem, contact Alcoholics Anonymous. AA is an informal society that operates in many countries and offers peer support for recovery from alcoholism.

Please visit https://www.aa.org/find-aa/world for more information.

ACKNOWLEDGMENTS

The storyline of this book was the first book I had ever written. It stemmed from my liking of crime documentaries and from seeing a particular crime in Australia, which planted the seed in my mind.

Plenty of people helped me make this book what it is. Thank you to Silvia, Samantha, the team at Proofreading Services for their exceptional editing, and Emily for her stunning book cover.

I'd like to thank my mom, who has been tremendously supportive and enthusiastic through my writing journey.

You might have noticed DJ Mesah. No, it is not made up—my friend DJs. She's amazing, so go check her out at www.soundcloud.com/dj_mesah.

A shout out to Linkin Park. Their music got me through the dark times in my life. RIP Chester.

To all the authors of the books I have read over the years, thank you! Thank you for the tears, the laughs, the excitement, and the frustration. To the nights that turned into days. Thank you for providing a safe place to escape from reality.

To the first few editors I had that had a pole stuck up their ass that weren't impressed with the themes of this book and made snarky little comments throughout the editing stage: *fuck you!* I'm proud of this book and I hope other people enjoy it too ☺

And to my readers, I cannot thank you enough for your support and patience.

Until next time,

Bianca Lee Ward

Bianca Lee Ward

ABOUT THE AUTHOR

Bianca Lee Ward is an Australian romance author with a love of culinary adventures and a playlist for every mood. She enjoys exploring themes of identity, personal growth, and resilience in her work—with a little spice on the side. When she isn't lost in storytelling or absorbed in her latest read, Bianca can be found watching true crime stories and documentaries.

You can connect with Bianca online at:
Website: www.biancaleeward.com
Email: info@biancaleeward.com
Instagram: https://www.instagram.com/biancaleeward
Facebook: https://www.facebook.com/biancaleeward
Spotify: Bianca Lee Ward
Pinterest: https://www.pinterest.com.au/biancaleeward
Goodreads: https://www.goodreads.com/author/show/30477361.Bianca_Lee_Ward
BookBub: https://www.bookbub.com/authors/bianca-lee-ward

Don't forget to sign up to Bianca's mailing list, where you'll get *huge* discounts, *exclusive* giveaways, and new release alerts!

www.ingramcontent.com/pod-product-compliance
Lightning Source LLC
Chambersburg PA
CBHW061118100726
47911CB00013B/592